BROKEN WEB

PATRICIA SNELLING

First published in 2017. Revised and reprinted in January 2020.

Published by Patricia Snelling, Inthelight Publishers
Auckland
New Zealand
patricia.snelling.books@gmail.com
Website: patriciasnelling.com

Scripture quotations are from the World English Bible

Martin Joyce Thoughtfields Graphic Design
Harold Joyce Front Cover Art Work

A catalogue record for this book is available from the National Library of New Zealand ISBN: 9780473396077

Books by Author:

When Hope Went South (Dart River Novel #1)

Jessie's High Country Heart (Dart River Novel #2)

Mack The Good Shepherd (Dart River Novel #3)

Missing On Kawau

Broken Web (Peace Haven Series#1)

Unshakable (Peace Haven Series#2) Published as Rescue Net 2017

Disclaimer
The novel is written using British English with New Zealand colloquialisms

Chapter One

Belle Spencer liked to daydream—in fact, she had a reputation for it and could think of nothing better on days off from her nursing job than to sink back into a couch with a cup of herbal tea, twiddling her toes and listening to the bellbirds in the garden—then she would close her eyes and wait.

Within minutes, a vision would often manifest in her mind. Is this a daydream—a message from God—or a figment of her wild imagination? She could never decide one way or the other.

In her vision is a lush, green farmlet with a nostalgic homestead covered in roses. This colonial farmhouse built in Oamaru stone is an original. The cosy home has eight bedrooms which open out onto a long veranda with white railings. There is a large farmhouse kitchen with a cast iron wood range—a perfect setting for a holistic retreat. She describes this perfectly in her journal each time the revelation occurs.

The small lake which abounds with ducks and geese is lined with huge willow trees and long wooden benches, strategically placed. Across the shallow river stretches a whitewashed, miniature, arched wooden bridge abundantly covered with climbing old-fashioned roses. Tall kowhai trees featuring bright yellow flowers line the pathway around the lake. It is picturesque and peaceful—the perfect spot for the weary guests coming to the lodge to heal. This retreat is a rural sanctuary for the "walking wounded", in need of a peaceful and loving environment to recover from their traumatic lives. It is a community, a well-known and sought after holistic sanctuary.

This vision began to manifest when she least expected it.

****

Belle was an avid member of the Outdoor Pursuits Club in Avonleigh, East Auckland for several years and loved getting away from hectic city life with the group for weekends, especially the long weekends.

She felt so alive when out at sea in her kayak with the warm breeze in her face and salt air filling her lungs or hiking through the abundant native forests, smelling the sweetness that emanated from the forest floor. This was when she felt closest to God.

This weekend was a four-day public holiday, and she was off to Randle's Cove near Waihi Beach in the Western Bay of Plenty.

Her club would meet up with the one from Winton Abbot, just over two hour's drive from Avonleigh.

Before she hit the highway in her Morris Minor with her tomato-red kayak on the roof-rack, she thanked her elderly neighbour, Mabel for taking care of Socks, her cat.

****

The first night at the lodge, weary from the drive down, Belle looked for a quiet spot where she could sit on the deck over-looking the sea. She sat with a bottle of her home-brewed ginger beer, listening to the wood pigeons and bellbirds and watching the sun go down. The impressive orange fireball sank slowly below the horizon.

She enjoyed being with the outdoor group, except for their boisterous drinking sessions when they revved up in the evenings. The atmosphere unsettled her, and she observed that the more alcohol they consumed, the louder their raucous laughter and more ridiculous nonsense they talked.

The following day, the coordinator gave everyone packed lunches for the trip and Belle headed off on the hike.

They set out to see the famous Fairy Falls Grove. The uphill hike proved a challenge for Belle as a result of having Polio as a child. Though she didn't have a limp, it was the breathing that got her mostly, but she wasn't going to let that hold her back,

3

stopping at regular intervals to sit on a rock and regain her strength.

****

'Mind if I share this hard seat with you to look at the view?' The gentle male voice came from behind.

Belle hesitated for a moment. 'Of course—be my guest.'

'Milton's my name.' He shook her hand and took a swig from his pump bottle.

'Belle—Belle Spencer. I'll take a while to catch the others up, although our leader won't let me out of her sight.'

'I can walk with you if you like. I don't believe in racing from start to finish as fast as possible without taking in the breath-taking views, or watching the amazing birds.'

Belle took a deep breath, savouring the sweet smell of the forest. 'You're right. We should be enjoying the forests and wildlife as well as the tranquillity. That's why I come to these places.'

'It's one thing that annoys me about these groups—the other is that too much drinking goes on at night.' His tone sounded indignant. I've found a friend! She stood up, adjusting her pack on her shoulders. 'We'd better catch up to the others. They are probably waiting for us further up.'

Milton led the way along the windy bush path. 'I can walk with you if you like for the rest of the weekend. Are you keen to do some abseiling?'

'Sure, but I've only done it once on a smaller climb—I think I'll wait till we get to the top to see how high it is.'

They followed the path alongside the gushing waterfall which became more spectacular the higher they climbed. The white foam glistened in the dazzling sunlight. On both sides of the waterfall, a native rain forest boasted towering kauri trees that hovered over the pathway and flamboyant parrots flocked to the trees for seeds.

As they approached the group to join them at the top, some were already unpacking their abseiling gear.

'I thought we were stopping for lunch first.' Belle mumbled within earshot of the leader.

The leader pointed in the direction of the shaded area. 'That's right—we're stopping here for lunch and we'll sit over there under the trees.'

Belle removed her jacket and dumped her backpack on the ground. 'Thank goodness for that!'

The leader took hold of her clipboard. 'I've told the group that those who want to can start abseiling with Mike, our experienced climber who'll be in charge of that group. I'll be with the ones who stay back for lunch and I need names now.'

Belle grinned, winking at Milton. 'That's good—I'll stick by Milton. I hear he is an experienced climber as well.'

After a few hours of sitting around eating and taking in the awesome views, they started to descend next to the waterfall.

Milton's protective nature sensed her trepidation. 'I'll help you get your harness on correctly—don't worry, I'll go down next to you. We have two ropes and the others are going down in twos.'

When they arrived safely below, Belle felt a huge sense of gratitude for Milton's help. He seemed different from the rest, and since she'd been on her own, she had not been able to find a man whom she could trust or respect. The few men Belle had dated since she'd been on her own were insincere and disrespectful, or they had ulterior motives and she gave up hope of ever meeting the right one—an honest man who didn't take advantage of her. Growing up with dysfunction in her family of origin, the behaviour became familiar to her—but now she was on a journey of becoming a whole person, learning about healthy intimacy and it had taken years and much heartache to recognise the difference.

I wonder if Milton is single. We seem to be on the same page, but perhaps he's a seasoned bachelor and doesn't want commitment. Oh, don't even go there! You know what your spiritual advisor said. When God sends Mr Right along, it will be when you least expect it.

Belle was fed up with waiting but she kept reminding herself that in the past, she jumped in too quickly with dire consequences, leaving serious wreckage in her life.

She continued to remonstrate with herself.

I've got used to being on my own and I mustn't get involved again in case I attract another disaster into my life.

Milton startled her with a tap on the shoulder. She hadn't noticed him watching her from afar.

'A penny for your thoughts—there's a spectacular view of the waterfall from the track across that bridge where we can get some good photos. Some of the others have gone there already.' He led the way.

Belle loved the outdoors, especially the birds. They gave her immense joy in life and she loved the way they flitted from branch to branch chirping happily—so full of enthusiasm for life.

This reminded her of home. Her bedroom was surrounded by trees full of birds. Before her alarm went off for work each morning, she would be woken by a chorus of bird song. There was always one song which stood out, one bird which seemed to sing a reply to the others. Another would join in, then another, until they formed a musical ensemble. This pattern repeated itself each morning. Belle believed it was sent to comfort her and aid healing. Her creator knew how much pain she was in as she'd been to hell and back.

Chapter Two

Milton fumbled around in his backpack for his camera. 'Belle,—I can hear the waterfall up ahead. We must be close now.'

Her face lit up. 'Look, there it is!'

He beamed a smile. 'Give me your camera—stand over there by that rock so I can take a photo of you with the waterfall in the background.'

'Sure, thanks—only if you let me take one of you too.' Belle felt uncomfortable, unsure of his motives. Why does he want a photo of me?

They starting walking back to the camp where they were staying. As they walked through the tree-studded forest surrounded by tall Redwoods, Belle found the courage to ask Milton if he was an old school friend she once knew at High School.

She had memories of herself at sixteen, a member of the youth orchestra playing her trumpet. A young lad would meet her after rehearsal and carry her instrument. Belle then drove him home in her mother's car and the boy's mother often invited her in for a cup of hot chocolate.

'Are you Milton from Bellevue—the one who biked twenty kilometres to see me in Winton Abbot one afternoon for high tea? I was sixteen, and you were fourteen.' Belle's cheeks flushed with nervousness as she made herself vulnerable. She had taken a risk.

'What! You aren't Belle Spencer from First Avenue are you— the one with the horses? I would never have guessed—wow!' He surreptitiously looked her up and down.

'Have I aged that much?' She smoothed her hair with her fingers.

'No, I didn't mean that—your hair was sunbleached and you were skinny. You'll have to tell me your life story. Are you married and do you have a family?'

He seemed to show considerable interest in her, to ask such questions.

'Not anymore. A lot of water has gone under my bridge, I'm afraid.' She exposed the sadness in her voice.

'A mostly painful past which I find hard to talk about.' Now she was starting to feel considerably uncomfortable.

'Me too. I hope you don't find me intrusive, but I've been to hell and back too. I'm on my own now but have two loving adult children, thank God. They're from my first marriage.' He appeared to be sensitive about his past.

Belle stopped to apply more sunscreen to her face and neck. 'You don't have to talk about it, I understand. If you're like me, you'll want to move on.'

They walked back down to the car park below, both keeping their counsel for the rest of the descent.

Belle pondered over all that they had discussed. She had suffered a traumatic past of domestic violence and going away on these outdoor pursuits contributed to her healing.

****

On the agenda the next day, was a paddle to Brown's Island, the wildlife sanctuary. They paid the leader for a packed lunch, which the coordinator handed out after breakfast.

At the sanctuary, the abundant bird-life—gannets, parrots, bellbirds, huge albatrosses and white herons sparked Belle's interest. Resting on a patch of grass, Belle and Milton ate their lunch while others went swimming. The sparkling blue water tempted Belle too. It was high tide, and she had remembered to wear her bathing suit under her shorts and tee-shirt.

Milton caught a glimpse of her rubbing sunscreen lotion on her athletic calves and thighs. Her strong, toned body was more than shapely for a woman in her early forties, acquired by the kayaking and horse riding she had done in her youth. He quickly

10

diverted his gaze as she approached him. 'Milton—are you coming in?'

'That depends how cold it is. I'm a bit of a wimp when it comes to cold water, and I saw you cringe when you got under.'

Belle dived under again. The water was unexpectedly warm and the tension in her neck left her while she floated on her back. 'Come on in Milton—it's so warm!'

He tiptoed towards the water and dived under, coming up with a huge grin. 'Wow! It sure is warm. It must be caused by the scorching heat on the sand all morning. That's unusual.' He dived under again.

Others started to join them in the freak warm current that only appeared to be in one spot. Belle and Milton didn't want to get out, but they had to get back before the tide went too low for their kayaks.

When they arrived on the mainland, a day of exercise, sun, and sea had tired Belle out. It was a great day, especially the companionship. I wonder if he has anyone back home.

That evening, some of the group started a card game, while others played scrabble. As they drank, they became noisy and loud and Belle needed some quiet time. She wandered onto the covered deck and sank down into a long pink couch with a ginger beer she'd brought from home.

As she sat peering out towards to the horizon, the evening mist descended over the sea while bellbirds sat chirping on the roof, as if they were saying goodnight. Seagulls made a nostalgic sound as they hovered overhead—a sound that took her back to her childhood when her family lived by the sea.

Milton appeared suddenly. He leaned over her, offering a bowl of potato crisps. 'Can I disturb your peace or are you wanting some space?'

'I'm just reminiscing. Places like this remind me of where I lived when I was young.'

He joined her on the couch. 'Your family home I visited when I biked over to see you, was near a beach like this.'

'Yes, that was the bay where I used to drag my canoe to on a trolley. Dad had made it from canvas strutted on a wooden frame. Amazing piece of work for a simple carpenter wasn't it?' She remembered her father with fondness.

They both sat reminiscing until midnight, sharing their personal stories. Belle told him she was fed up with relationships, as none of them had worked out, and she didn't think she would marry again. Milton told her he felt the same way.

'We've both experienced a lot of hurt in our lives, and there is only so much pain a person can handle, don't you think?'

Belle didn't respond to him and went quiet again. Yet, unbeknown to both of them, at this point, a special bond was forming between them, because they had been childhood sweethearts for a time.

Milton prodded her gently on her arm. 'Do you remember what it was that caused us to fall out back then?'

She took out a handkerchief to wipe the drip that formed on her nose. 'Yes, I do. I drove you home after a Youth Orchestra concert in Mum's Morris Mini. When I pulled up at your gate, you leaned over and tried to plant a big smacker on my lips. I was horrified, at sixteen! I mean, in those days that was pretty risqué.'

'That's right!' Milton burst out laughing. 'You pushed me out the door fast and took off like Atom Ant!' He laughed again, affectionately.

'Then you tried to track me down when I was a First-Year student at Auckland Hospital. You poor thing—you were so brave coming to the nurses' residence asking for me.' Belle's neck flushed with the memory of this.

'And when I asked for you at Reception, you had an entourage of nursing friends shielding you from unwanted admirers, of which I was one, I think. You were just a normal seventeen-year-old girl by then, but I took it so personally.'

'Ooh, that sounds terrible—I wasn't really that horrid, just scared of being loved. If anyone was genuine and really cared about me, it was unfamiliar and risky. I couldn't cope with emotionally available men like you. I was only used to emotionally unavailable men in my childhood home and relationships.'

'I understand—we were both just young and immature.'

'I'm so sorry if I caused you any harm, Milton. Young boys can be sensitive to rejection.'

'No harm was done—I've had plenty of other girlfriends in my time, so let's move on.' He had a hint of sadness in his tone.

'I've changed now, but in those days I was only drawn to drunks and rogues. Later in life, I longed for a stable, solid relationship with a genuinely decent man, but it never happened.'

Belle felt awkward. She got up and went out to the kitchen to get them both a bottle of ginger beer. They sat together until it was time to go to their respective bunk rooms.

'I'll catch you at breakfast before we pack up and leave. It's been so good chatting and walking to the waterfall with you today Belle. I hope we can meet up again after we leave here.'

That night, when Belle climbed into her sleeping bag, she spent hours tossing and turning feeling regret, deep regret that she had let Milton go when she was seventeen years old.

Most people at that age don't have committed relationships— how stupid of me! Why didn't I end up marrying someone like Milton? Now it's too late—the chance of me meeting anyone decent and worth marrying is so remote.

A deep sense of hopelessness sank like a rock in the pit of her soul that she would have to face being alone for the rest of her days.

****

Next morning, her roommate, Sonya chastised her as she awoke. 'Belle—come on, wakie, wakie! It's time to get up and the breakfast gong has gone. Unless you want to miss breakfast, which is unlike you, Miss Foodie.'

Belle woke remembering that Milton had arranged to have breakfast with her and she didn't want to miss out, especially as they were leaving that morning.

'Hey, I'm coming.' She yanked up her denim jeans that matched her royal blue blouse and raced a brush through her sandy coloured hair. 'I'll shower after breakfast—I'm coming now.'

Milton sat sipping coffee in an agitated state, looking as if he'd been stood up.

'I'm so sorry—I slept in and nearly missed breakfast—the girls woke me.'

He smiled. 'No worries, I'm glad you turned up.' He leaned forward over the table. 'I wanted to say it was really great to see you after all these years and I've enjoyed your company.' He reached for her hand. 'Would you mind if I look you up in the next few weeks? I let you go once, and won't let that happen so easily this time.'

'Yes of course—it was amazing to meet you too after so many years. This weekend was fabulous, especially how we talked and shared.'

Milton leaned over and whispered, 'Meet me in the carpark after you've packed up and we can swap contact details if you wish.'

'Absolutely! Belle uttered—I'll be there at ten.'

Later that morning, Milton waited for her in the carpark on the dot of ten with pen and notebook in hand.

'If you write down your number, I'll contact you about meeting up in Winton Abbot if you like.' They swapped numbers and addresses and Milton gave her a hand to carry her bags to the car.

'We'll have to keep in touch,' he said. 'I'll send you some of the photos I took on the hikes.'

'I'd love that. I'll bring some photos of my family when I see you in Winton Abbot. I'm playing my trumpet with my concert band soon and I'll send you a ticket if you would like to come to that.'

Milton helped load her kayak onto the roof-rack and waved her off as she headed home.

While driving back to Auckland, she started daydreaming, and couldn't believe what took place over the weekend. She pondered it all the way home.

By the end of the week, she'd received a letter from her new man to say he looked forward to meeting her again and how much their talks had meant to him.

****

Milton worked from home in Winton Abbot—counselling and mentoring local farmers who were struggling with serious issues. His family had a long heritage of farming.

The past few years he'd cared for his sick mother who'd moved off the farm to live in Winton Abbot when his father died. When his mother passed away, he inherited her stately home and used one of the rooms as an office when he set up his counselling business.

When farming took a downturn, he was offered a contract with Federated Farmers working as a counsellor with farmers in crisis. He enjoyed the great outdoors—that's when he felt close to God.

****

Belle wanted to slow this down. Suddenly she had cold feet and felt terrified of rushing in. She decided to go to Otago to see her daughter Rose and husband, Andy on their high-country sheep station. She had arranged to help them out—mainly with cooking dinners and baking for the shearing gang while their cook was away on leave.

'Mum! We would love to see you. I'll send you your air ticket. You are not paying for it when you always end up working for us.'

Chapter Three

Belle enjoyed being with her daughter as she didn't get to see her often enough. The return fare wasn't cheap, and Rose and Andy could seldom get time away, except if their relief farm manager was able to fill in for them.

While staying with Rose at Perendale Station, she tried hard not to think about Milton, but his kind, caring character, the bond they formed and the fun they had swimming at Randle's Cove, stayed uppermost in her mind. It bothered her that she couldn't detach from the memories of their eventful weekend.

'Mum, you seem to be away with the fairies. Come on—I'm taking the jeep into Wanaka to stock up. We can go for a coffee somewhere and I need a break away from here for a while.'

Belle stood checking her wallet for her cash.

'Sounds great Rose. If there are any dress shops there, perhaps I could get you a new summer blouse if we can find anything suitable. I've also brought my chequebook.'

Belle had a wonderful time at Perendale with Rose and Andy. She helped Rose make new drapes, as her daughter had no time for domestic tasks working on the farm. She had missed Rose so much since she'd moved south and married Andy who had grown up on a large farm near the lakes.

Rose rarely saw her brothers, but they both visited her a few times a year, as Rose wasn't able to get away from the busy working station and it was easier for her family to visit her.

When Belle returned to Avonleigh, there was a message on her answer-phone from Milton which took her by surprise, as he knew she'd gone south with Rose.

'Hi Belle, it's Milton. Just in case you'd forgotten about me while you were with your daughter, I thought you might be missing the sound of my voice haha. Check your mail as I've just sent you a note. Talk soon, shall we? Bye for now.'

It surprised Belle to hear from him so soon, but she knew in her heart that she'd missed him—their intimate discussions and deep sharing they did while away at the adventure weekend. She couldn't wait to get to the mailbox.

After she finished unpacking and got out her uniform ready for work, she checked her mail

There it was with a subject heading—

I'm So Lonesome I Could Cry, Du Wa Du Wa.

Hi Belle

Isn't it time we met up again—what do you think?

I was worried you might forget all about me in the deep South. I hope not!

I'd like you to come down and visit me in Winton Abbot to check out where I live, and I'll pay for your accommodation in the Bed and Breakfast place near my home. That way, there wouldn't be any gossip from my church or accusations of "hanky-panky" from the elders who live at the end of my street. Let me know what you think. If you don't want to drive down, I can shout you the fare on the shuttle bus. They have a special on now.

There is a great wildlife park here with an amazing café, where I'd like to take you for lunch. Please say yes!

I can drive you back on Sunday, or even better, you could ask your boss if you can have the Monday off, and I can drive you back home after the weekend. I have some business to do in Auckland, so it will work out well.

Blessings and fond thoughts

Milton

****

Milton knew all about grief, loss and pain being widowed twice. His first wife died of pancreatic cancer from alcoholism after ten difficult years. His second wife, Gabriel, was killed when her car hit a tractor on a country road. She'd been the perfect match for Milton and left him with two children.

Gabby, his daughter, named after her mother lives in the Nelson Lakes with husband, Russell the Park Ranger. She has a degree in Environmental Science.

Tyler, an Orthopaedic Specialist, is married to a Canadian girl called Elly in Toronto. Their three-year-old son, Max, looks so much like Milton, and their daughter, Milly is named after her grandfather and has just started school.

Milton's counselling role involves working with troubled farmers in the province suffering extreme stress due to severe droughts and low milk prices. It has been the worst on record for many years.

****

Each year, Belle attends a weekend Christian camp in the Thames Valley, where she catches up with old friends. The camp lies about the same distance from Auckland and Winton Abbot and is usually a fun-packed weekend.

One morning while relaxing on her couch reading the church notice about the upcoming camp and checking the enrolment details, the phone rang.

'Good morning, Princess. What are you up to this weekend? I thought we could take a drive into the country if you can think of somewhere interesting. What do you say?'

Her words tumbled down the phone describing the details of the camp.

'Honestly, Milton there is so much going on there—it's right up your alley.'

'Mmm, I'm intrigued—go on.'

'The sizeable log-style lodge has male and female bunk rooms that sleep six, but usually, they're not all full. One of the members of the committee usually cooks for the weekend.'

'That sounds good, a break from my own grub.'

'Not far from the lodge are freshwater swimming holes that are not for the faint-hearted, as they're ice cold. The flying fox is popular with the younger ones.'

'So why do you think this is right up my alley?' Milton teased.

'It's the great outdoors you like so much—remote and beautiful with native trees, bush and wildlife.'

'Easy on girl—I was just kidding. I've heard about that camp, but never had the opportunity to go. Now I have good companionship, I could take the plunge. Drop me a line with all the details and what I need to pack. If you tell me over the phone, I'm likely to forget something important.'

That evening, before sleep took her hostage, Belle reminisced about the last camp she had attended. At night, when all was still except for the sound of cicadas, possums would put on a show right outside the bunkroom door. They took turns shimmying up and down the bannisters of the rustic veranda.

The baby possums fascinated Belle, trying to mimic their mothers. This was something she would never have seen in the city, the reason for her wanting to return each time.

****

Milton set off with his car packed to the hilt. The three-hour trip took him through the forest park ending on a windy, gravel road to the camp. Belle met him on arrival and showed him around.

That night, Possum, the volunteer cook from the previous year commandeered the kitchen—an eccentric man in his forties with a long, curly moustache. Belle eyed him suspiciously. 'What is that stew you're making for us tonight, Possum?'

'It's possum tonight, full of local herbs and lots of other goodies.'

She thought he was just kidding, but others assured her it really was possum stew—hearty and tasty they said. I shouldn't have asked.

Milton poked Belle playfully in the ribs. 'Umm—are you sure we have arrived at the right place?'

She kissed him on the cheek. 'If you're hungry, you'll eat whatever you are given.'

Milton, like Belle, was in his element. He had confided in her that he visualised running a place like this himself, but it was just a fleeting thought, he said.

Chapter Four

The next day, after a full day's hike and cooling off in one of the waterholes in the forest, Belle and Milton stretched out on the grass under the Rimu trees. Parched from the scorching sun, they sat drinking Belle's ginger beer they brought with them in the chilly bin.

'Belle—you said you would tell me your life story. I guess it's a sensitive subject, but I think it important for us to be transparent with each other, especially if we're contemplating a serious relationship.'

'I can do that but be prepared for a long-winded story.'

'Good—I enjoy long, drawn-out cliff-hangers,' he said, elbowing her.

She tore open a muesli bar and reached for her drink bottle, taking a few minutes to compose herself and then began.

'I spent years trying to find my lost identity, due to the deception of my parents. My mother, Elsie was married to my stepfather, Bernie—a man whom she later discovered was homosexual after he returned from the Second World War. He was also an alcoholic—a drop- down drunk.

In the house across the road, my biological father, Henry lived with his mother, Nina, a good friend of my own mum. When Nina started dying of leukaemia, she asked my mother if she would take care of Henry once she died.'

Belle hesitated, unsure if Milton could keep up.

'Look—this is complicated—are you following?'

'No problem, Belle. My years of counselling experience have put me in good stead— keep going—it's an interesting story so far.'

'Well—take care of Henry, she certainly did. Nina died and there they were, two bereaved souls consoling each other. Elsie and Bernie invited Henry to move in with them. I was born out of this union. All my life, I was raised in the guise of my stepfather's child. I was the apple of Henry's eye who treated me as such— though I never understood why.'

'Hold on Belle—I'll just grab another cold drink from the chilly bin.' Milton reapplied sunscreen lotion and sat down with his drink, handing Belle a glass.

He elbowed her. 'Please continue with the story—it's starting to get juicy.'

'The family made a sudden exodus to Winton Abbot from Auckland to hide their shameful existence from the neighbours when my mother was about to give birth. I was born in a tiny rural maternity clinic, outside Winton Abbot while we were living on our friends' farm where my father worked as a farm labourer.

Bernie separated from my mother and took to the hills with a share-milking partner who was also a chronic alcoholic. A year later, his partner left him high and dry abandoning him and clearing out their joint bank account, leaving him with nothing.

During this time, Elsie and Henry had a house built in town for themselves. They were a happy little family, the couple with their newborn baby and five-year-old Will whom Elsie and Bernie had adopted. Their own son, Charles who was ten years my senior, lived as a boarder at King's private school in Remuera, Auckland.

After Bernie was left in ruin, he suffered a nervous breakdown. Elsie and Henry couldn't abandon him in that state, and out of mercy, took him in. Thereafter, the three had an arrangement that they would live together in a kind of symbiotic relationship with Elsie and Henry carrying on their relationship discreetly, while Bernie chose to live in a separate building on our property. Quite bizarre.'

Belle shivered. 'I think I'll go behind those bushes and change out of my wet bathing suit. I won't be long.'

Within minutes she sat back down and huddled next to Milton.

'Are you sure you want me to continue—it's a long and drawn out story—I can tell you the rest another time.'

Milton wrapped his arms around her shoulders.

'No, please keep going—it's like a mystery unfolding—I want to hear the end now.' He gave her a broad smile.

'They all lived with the most enormous deception—a tangled web. Every time my mother accompanied Henry to leave town on holiday, it was always without her husband. When out of town, they drilled me to lie and tell people Henry was my father and use his surname—but when we were at home in Winton Abbot, I was to use Bernie's surname and say that he was my father. I was forced to live a double life, to live a lie.'

Milton appeared puzzled. 'Wow, Belle—it certainly is a tangled web! How did they manage to keep up such a pretence—a charade?'

'It gets a lot worse. The thing is—I didn't know the truth. They kept it from me, but I instinctively knew there was something wrong and always wondered if I had been adopted.

I was led to believe that Bernie was my father all through my childhood, while the whole time my real father was nurturing me and caring for me as a real father would. He was always there for me as my guardian, right under my nose.'

'Man that is so cruel,—withholding the truth I mean.'

'In my late thirties, after drilling my family with questions, I began to realise Bernie wasn't my father. During my teens, I began to question if I had been adopted, as he and I had never bonded nor had I any kind of relationship. He would seldom engage with me.'

'That must have been confusing for you. Your stepfather was obviously emotionally unavailable.'

As Belle started to shiver, Milton placed his jacket over her shoulders.

'When I started my journey of enlightenment during my early thirties, I started thinking about Henry, how good he was to me—such happy memories. A voice inside me said I needed to find him, but my mother refused to tell me where he was. When I eventually found out, she resented me visiting him and became angry when I mentioned his name. That's because he'd married a woman who was a family friend and later became her rival, competing for my father's attention. My mother had a right to be bitter, I suppose.'

Milton handed her a plate with cake. 'Here, Belle, have a mug of coffee and some of this cake that Possum somehow conjured up. Carry on—I'm keen to hear how your search for him panned out.' He poured coffee from a thermos.

'Thanks.' She continued, 'One weekend I visited old family friends, Betty and George in Winton Abbot who'd known Henry for many years. I told them I had the gut feeling that Henry was my father and I was searching for him. Betty said that I should trust my gut feelings and insisted I visit him and gave me his address. She told me Henry had been married to this woman for thirty years!'

'Well thank God for Betty—what a good lead!'

'When I turned up on his doorstep in Winton Abbot, his wife Moira was at the door. She was surprised but not obnoxious, as I did not announce myself as his daughter—not yet—just a friend and was no threat at that point.

Henry acted awkward towards me and asked why I was there, which hurt deeply. He relaxed and later in the day when Moira was in the kitchen, he furtively showed me something. It was a large book called Racing Bible for goodness' sake! He opened it towards the middle and showed me a photo of both of us together when I was about fourteen years old. He showed me another he had hidden away. I was shocked that he felt he had to hide them.

After that visit, I used to see him regularly, driving down from Auckland to Winton Abbot once a month. Sometimes I took him out for a meal or a drive in the country and as we grew closer, Moira became jealous.

When I tried to phone him from home, Moira usually answered the phone curtly and never passed on my messages. I posted him cards and letters which never reached him.

Once, I was on holiday staying with my friend in Winton Abbot when paid Henry a visit. Moira came to the door with a poker face spitting her words out that I was not welcome and to stay away. Naturally, I was devastated.

My father cowered as he towered over this small, spiteful woman distressed and tearful, saying he was sorry— that it would be better for me to keep away as Moira is getting upset!'

Milton burst forth, 'That is incredibly manipulative and selfish—what an awful woman!'

'I was gutted that Moira had bullied him into isolating me. I knew he had post-traumatic stress from the war and hated conflict, but that didn't alleviate my pain.

Well, they say—"what goes around comes around", as the woman was diagnosed with cancer shortly after, and died within a year. Henry must have loved her, as her death destroyed him.

He wanted me to move down to Winton Abbot which I did. After he was on his own, I had long-awaited, quality time with him for two years before he died.

I miss him now but feel grateful that I reunited with him and for the special time we had—although I still feel robbed of all those years I missed out on a father-daughter relationship. My children were robbed of their grandfather's input in their lives too.'

'How were you sure that he was your biological father?'

'I made sure Moira wasn't going to rob me of my rightful relationship with him. During those two years, just to uphold my birthright we both undertook a DNA test which proved that Henry was my father.'

Belle continued eager to finish the story and move on.

'Another negative impact on my life, and to put it mildly, a huge dilemma of all this was the loss of identity all those years.

My parents had lived a double life of incredible deception, and to compound this—I too became full of denial. I was so lost and had to start rebuilding my life again after that but attracted abusive men who were full of deceit. It was a vicious circle of lies and deception.

My father's relatives, though I had met some of them during my childhood, treated me as the black sheep. They didn't want me to talk about my father or the past. They were in denial and would rather I stayed invisible—hoping I would not let any of the skeletons out of the cupboard.'

Milton stroked her arm. 'How on earth did you manage to stay sane through it all— where do you get your strength?'

'I went on a kind of spiritual pilgrimage, one of self- discovery, and booked into various holistic retreats where I could meditate in peace and quiet and do journaling. There were a few good counsellors, but I also had one or two spiritual advisors who helped me most.

My life really changed when I attended one of those Alpha Courses run by Nicky Gumbel—an Anglican programme to help people come to grips with their Christian faith. It changed my life.'

'I did a couple of those too and they are marvellous,' said Milton.

'I was virtually nurtured back to wholeness and the icing on the cake was the programme called Restoring Past Foundations. This is something that I'd like to be involved in—you know — helping others who have been to hell and back on the pathway to healing.'

'Belle, I really appreciate you sharing these deeply personal details of your life—it's a real privilege to hear this.'

Belle wrapped her arms around herself. 'I'm starting to get cold and the sun is going down.' She started gathering her things together. 'I expect we'd better get on back,'

'Keep my jacket on. I have my sweatshirt.' Milton picked up the chilly bin and as they starting walking back, he took her hand as they wandered along the dirt road that led to the lodge, both deep in thought.

Chapter Five

Two years later, three months after a simple wedding, Belle and Milton sat in the front garden of Milton's family home in Winton Abbot, planning their future.

Belle waved a Real Estate magazine in front of Milton.

'Look at these photos—here it is—the exact property we've been looking for! It's like the one I keep seeing in my vision.'

Milton picked up his calculator. 'Mmm—it's rather beyond our budget, don't you think? We may not have enough.'

Belle went over the figures in her head.

'I can sell my rental property in Auckland—I don't want to hold on to it as it's too much hassle trying to keep an eye on it when we live so far away.'

'Okay, then. We can contact the agent in the morning to ask when she can show us through. In the meantime let's find out how much your property is worth and I'll contact my bank. I'll put my house on the market and see what we're left with.'

Belle became like an excited school girl. 'Woohoo—I can't wait.'

****

A few weeks later, Belle and Milton became the ecstatic and grateful owners of a beautiful farmlet with a lodge they called Peace Haven—a forty-minute drive from Winton Abbot in picturesque Cromwell Mead on lush, rural land in Hauraki near Athenree.

There it was, just as Belle had envisioned—an English country-style lodge on five acres of park-like grounds built of stone from the local quarry. The long, white veranda looked out towards a picture post-card view of the ranges. Inside the lodge, all eight double bedrooms came with Ensuite—four upstairs and four down and there were separate quarters for the owners.

Peace Haven drew people from, not only their local community but also from all over New Zealand.

There was the lonely burnt-out businessman, drawn to the wholesome home-cooked food and uplifting company like a bee to a honey pot.

Each month a widow turned up who disappeared each day to sit on a park bench by the little bridge talking to the geese and smelling the roses. She'd sit for hours staring into the water while Belle and Milton often wondered what she thought about, as she always returned to the homestead full of smiles and in a trance-like relaxed state.

They hired a part-time chef they called Cookie who could prepare wholesome meals utilising the fresh vegetables and herbs from their expansive, organic garden. The smell of fresh-baked bread wafting through from the kitchen each morning became a real favourite amongst the guests. The chef even made cottage cheese from the milk he swapped with the neighbour for Peace Haven's vegetables and eggs.

Belle also used her exemplary culinary skills to help in the kitchen such as her natural yoghurt and sourdough bread. When strawberries were in season, her strawberry jam was a special hit with their Devonshire teas and hot scones. During summer, another favourite was Belle's fresh berry ice-cream, made from her organically grown strawberries, raspberries and blueberries. She spent her free time with the miniature ponies she had bred—a popular feature at Peace Haven, and once a month, she gave free pony rides to the children from the local village.

****

At the end of a hot day, Belle often sat under the awning of on their veranda in her favourite chair gazing out at the sunset while reflecting on her life. In the cool of the evening, she'd view the small lake in the distance, admiring the dark red roses at the water's edge. She could almost hear a pin drop in the stillness—

37

what bliss, as she'd sit mesmerised by the sun—a bright orange ball sinking slowly behind the hills. It warmed her up on the inside, as she would imagine God's immense light looking something like this.

As she reflected on her past, she ruminated on the patterns of her life that had caused her to get involved in past destructive relationships. Her need to rescue needy, dysfunctional men—did it come from her bizarre childhood and upbringing, or was it something more sinister—something spiritual? Whenever she fell in love with a man, it always turned to custard, as though it was doomed to happen. Perhaps it was some generational curse that had caused such mayhem in her life. Then she recalled a verse she once read in her bible—Therefore, if anyone is in Christ, he is a new creation. The old things have passed away. Behold, all things have become new.

Now things were different, as she'd begun a whole new chapter in her life—the foundation for a positive and happy future. There was no turning back now for Belle, as she was determined to never allow toxic people to enter her life again. The land that the locusts had eaten was slowly being restored, just as God had promised.

Milton interrupted her private spiritual space lovingly stroking her hair. 'Time for a cuppa? I'll put the billy on and join you before the sun goes down.'

'Grab some of those fruit muffins from the tin, Milton—I don't think I'll last till dinner time—not after my gardening session this afternoon, it usually makes me ravenous.'

They drank their tea from dainty Royal Albert cups and watched the changing technicolour of the sun setting on the horizon.

Milton pulled out his notebook. 'I had a phone call from a lady in Lake Taupo who booked a room for ten days. She has just left a violent marriage.'

'Oh, poor thing—how old is she?' Belle felt a chill go down her spine, an echo from the past.

'She told me her children are in their early thirties, so I'm guessing late fifties or sixties.'

'I'll put her in the Camelia Suite—it's quiet and sunny and will lift her spirit.'

'Says she is a trained chef and would like to volunteer to help Cookie if she can be of any use which will keep her mind off her problems.'

'That's a wonderful idea, love, as Cookie has a funeral to attend and I'll be slaving over a hot stove by myself—so that works well. I might learn a thing or two from her.'

****

Christmas came around too fast, and a few days before Christmas day, Belle ran around like a chook with its head off preparing for the arrival of their family about to descend on them for the summer holidays.

Peace Haven closed during this period to give Milton and Belle time with their loved-ones and Belle had so much on her to-do list. She rushed around the bedrooms placing mini vases of fresh flowers on the bedside dressers which was her special touch.

Milton's son, Tyler tried to get over for Christmas, if he could get away with his family.

Rose and Andy came once a year when their farm manager took over the running of their sheep station of two thousand acres while they came to stay at Peace Haven for a break— although not always at Christmas.

Belle's son, Harry and wife, Anna live in Auckland in the quiet suburb of Northcote Point where they catch the ferry to the city to work each day. Harry works for himself as a project manager in the building industry. They love to get out of Auckland and enjoy country life, especially at Peace Haven.

Jimmy owns his own business as an Electronics Technician, and his wife Penny works in a Childcare Centre on the North Shore in Torbay. They also like to have a break hectic city life and spend time at the lodge. Penny spends most of her time riding the bay mare when she is there.

****

Milton drove his 12-seater passenger van to pick up the family from the airport. It meant a long round trip from the airport to the bus station and back to the airport.

Tyler and Elly arrived first with Max and Milly in tow. They had the long haul from Canada, and all crashed into bed before dinner.

Rose arrived at the airport from the South later that night with Andy who was relieved to see Milton standing next to the 12-seater van, waving at them. He was ravenous— a typical farmer with a hearty, farmer's appetite.

Jimmy and Penny waited for Milton at the Bus Station, as he was delayed at the airport earlier, and wasn't there to meet them straight away.

****

The next morning Max woke everyone at the crack of dawn racing around asking for his porridge, eager to get outside to feed the miniature ponies, where he spent most of his time each holiday.

Belle longed for her own grandchildren, and Milton's Max and Milly were the only ones they shared and she spoilt them rotten.

She started clearing the dining table. 'Guess what we're planning today, children.'

Max raced his plate into the kitchen with Milly in close pursuit. 'What's that, Grandma? I want to feed the ponies.'

'You have plenty of time to do that and when we all finish breakfast we're going for a walk to the lagoon. The blackberries are ripe, and if you help me fill the buckets, I'm going to bake us a huge blackberry pie.'

'Yummm! With clotted cream?' Max pleaded.

'Yes, I think we can manage that. Grandpa collected a whole bucket of cream from the neighbour yesterday, and I clotted it and kept it just for you.'

'Woohoo—can't wait—let's go'. Milly tugged on Belle's skirt.

'I have to cook breakfast for everyone first. Would you like to have a change from porridge? I'm cooking eggs and bacon, or French toast with banana for those who want it.'

Max grabbed Belle's sleeve and pointed at the freezer.

'And icecream—please, Grandma'.

Milly sat at the Bay window with her nose on the sill, gazing at her favourite pony.

Gabby and Russell arrived on a later flight that day. By mid-morning, the families were ready to set off for the lagoon, their favourite picnic spot during summer. They packed wicker hampers with cold, home-made lemonade, roast lamb, salads, freshly baked sourdough, blueberry muffins and fruit.

They all carried something, especially their swimming togs. Milton stored a folded Gazebo under the willow trees for such events. Elly kept a close eye on the children near the lagoon, although it had a shallow area where they could paddle.

After lunch, the rest of the family stretched out like beached whales while Belle took the children by the hand to go berry picking. They returned an hour later with a substantial amount of berries, sufficient for a large pie.

Elly stood gaping at her son. 'Max, your face is blue! I think you've eaten more than you've put in the bucket. I hope you won't be sick later.'

He patted his stomach. 'Yup, my tummy is full now.'

Tyler was already in the lagoon while Harry and Jimmy sat on a large branch overhanging the water. They wrestled and laughed their heads off, while the women sunned themselves in their colourful bikinis.

At dinner time, back at the lodge, they all chipped in to help out and then sat down to a fine meal. Belle lapped up the great compliments she received about her fresh berry ice-cream, which went well with the blackberry pie.

'Time for bed, Max, come on—it's getting late and you have a big day tomorrow if you want to ride the ponies.' Elly pulled him away from the sofa in the lounge. 'You can't fall asleep here'.

He resisted. 'I wanna say goodnight to Horace my special pony.' Elly's frustration level rose. 'Horace is sound asleep like you should be now.'

Max capitulated reluctantly.

The next morning, the men went with Milton to attend to a handful of sheep that needed shearing. Milton had grown up on a farm in the south and wanted to demonstrate his knowledge, although Andy was a seasoned sheep farmer. The wool from the small herd would be sent to a local craft guild which processed it for craft shops and various retailers to make garments.

Belle walked off with Milly and Max to pick bunches of fresh flowers for the lodge and returned with stunning azure-blue delphiniums, bright orange gerberas, mini white chrysanthemums, scarlet roses and sweet-smelling Asian Lillies. They gathered a small bouquet together to take to Annie to brighten up her lounge.

'You take them to her, both of you. Just knock on the door—she's in there and would love to see you.

Milly stood at her door, a real picture in her cornflour-blue, flared dress holding the bouquet with Max in tow.

'Oh Milly, that's so sweet, thank you. Come on in—I've something for you and Max.'

Annie had been busy making the children gingerbread men decorated with coloured chocolate buttons.

'Did you make those just for us? Thank you, Aunty Annie. Can I show them to Mummy? She tried to make some, but they didn't work out and just kept breaking.'

Milly grabbed the biscuit tin with the gingerbread and rushed off towards the door.

'Milly, you and Max can help me collect the eggs later if your mum says it's okay,' Annie called after them. She was so happy to be involved in Milton's grandchildren's lives as she began to feel at home at Peace Haven.

Christmas day was special at the lodge. They decorated the lounge two days before and Belle brought out a nativity scene each year for the children to see.

The characters and animals in the scene had been created from special wood, exquisitely formed. A round wooden turntable encircled by red tea-light candles created the power to turn it.

It fascinated Max. 'Make it go again Grandma, please.'

'Careful, Max—you can look but don't touch or it will break.'

She brought out a roll of crepe paper and plonked it on the dining table. 'Come on both of you—I want to show you how to make paper chains from my coloured, crepe paper. After that, you can ask your father if he could put them up around the lounge and dining room.'

When they returned home from church on Christmas day, they all found some way of unwinding and relaxing after another delicious home-cooked meal of Belle's. It was a peaceful and happy event.

****

After Christmas when the family had left Peace Haven, Belle felt a sense of loss for a short time—especially with her daughter living so far south and seeing her only once a year.

Fortunately, her boys did not live too far away to be able to drive to visit for a day, so they usually drove down for Christmas.

Milton also missed Tyler, naturally, but didn't mention it to Belle often. He planned to take Belle on a trip to Canada and booked a cruise to Alaska and Vancouver Islands with the Tyler and his family. It would be their first cruise ever.

****

As the years went by, Belle realised just how much she'd been living by the Grace of God who had really taken care of her—she was convinced of that.

The news on the television about global violence and terrorism, especially children being used as human bombs sickened her. Child abuse and domestic violence as well as natural disasters—even in her own land. What a mess the whole planet was in.

She sat on the veranda one evening pondering these issues and decided there had to be a way that one could attain happiness and have some kind of peace of mind through all this mayhem.

She came to the realisation that happiness is fleeting, only transient, and it is joy and faith that enables one to survive the terrible trials of this life in the end.

Joy is an inside job, she believed. Something that can well up from the inside in spite of the storms of life. It can happen when we perfectly trust God to do for us what we cannot do for ourselves when we are rendered completely powerless—even in the midst of the storms.

When I struggle and strive, I allow fear to enter and this kills joy, she kept telling herself.

Belle came to realise during her times of meditation, that acceptance is the pathway to peace, acceptance of life on life's terms, not her own terms.

Letting go and letting God is the key, she realised. But, to actually do so is a huge step. Sometimes life kicks us in the belly so hard, that all we can do is surrender, she reasoned as she watched the sun slowly hide its face behind the crest of the silhouetted hills.

Chapter Six

Milton walked up the steps and called out to Belle who stood in the dining room dusting a lampshade.

'Belle—where are you—oh, there you are. I thought you might like to come and pick mushrooms with me. It would be great to have some for breakfast. I've seen them popping up all over the place after the warm rain we had last night.'

'Good idea—I'll just put my walking shoes on and grab a sunhat. Where did you find them?'

'On the ridge by the neighbour's boundary fence. I thought they were daisies until I walked closer.'

'Mmm—I can smell them cooking now. I've got some bacon in the fridge we can have with them and plenty of rocket in my herb garden.'

'Hold on—the phone's ringing.' Milton took the call and poked his head through the dining-room door. 'It's Nancy—the woman who made a booking for the next week.'

'She's due until next Monday, right?'

'Yes, but she is asking if she can bring her little Bichon Frise dog. She said she'll keep him on a lead and won't let him chase the sheep or the hens.'

'As long as she takes care of him and keeps him on the veranda outside her room at night as he can't sleep in the bedrooms. People will complain if they smell dog in their rooms.'

'Okay, I'll let her know. I must ask her if she has any food preferences, as she didn't put it on the form.'

****

Nancy arrived the following week with Charlie, her dog and appeared relieved to have a break, as she needed to get some perspective on her life while at Peace Haven. She recently moved out of her home with a protection order in place after her husband had beaten her.

Belle and Milton showered her with tender, loving care until she was strong enough to go to her new home to live alone.

During the month that Nancy was at Peace Haven, her friend Sally, who was recently widowed, came to stay for a few weeks. She had been the main carer for her husband who had recently died of cancer after a long and arduous road.

One morning, Sally wandered through the fields at leisure admiring the array of coloured butterflies that frequented Peace Haven. She spent hours walking around taking photos of them or the animals. This time, she was mesmerised by a beautiful butterfly which she followed into the orchard oblivious to a warning sign on the gate.

Milton, donned in protective attire, had just collected honey from the half-dozen beehives he kept in the orchard. The bees encircled him as they normally did when starting walking back to the house. He caught a glimpse of Sally a short distance away. When he looked again—she appeared distressed as though she was trying to attract his attention, frantically flailing her hands in the air. Milton ran over to her to see what the commotion was about.

'What is it Sally—what's happening?'

'I think I've been stung by a bee while I was tried to take a close-up photo. My throat feels tight and my hands are beginning to swell.'

'Quickly, come to the house—I'll call Belle—she knows how to treat this.'

By the time they'd got inside the house, strange noises came from Sally as she tried to take a breath. Her lips had swelled and Milton took her pulse. 'Your heart is pounding.'

Belle was on the ball when they arrived. 'Are you allergic to bees that you know of?'

She shook her head and in between gasps, her voice croaked, as she answered, 'I can't remember being allergic ... but now I come to think of it ... when I was about seven ... my parents had to rush me to the doctor after a bee stung me.'

'Milton—quickly call an ambulance and then ring Doctor Bartlett down the road—he may get here sooner.'

Doctor Bartlett gave instructions to Belle over the phone, to give the medication she had in her emergency box.

'Sally—you are having a severe allergic reaction called anaphylaxis and you need a shot of adrenaline!' Belle advised.

'Do I have your permission to administer adrenaline—the antidote via an Epipen? It's quite safe, and it will reverse this toxic reaction—I'm a registered nurse.'

'Please—do whatever you need to. I don't mind as long as it helps,' she muttered between gasps.

'I'm going to inject it into the muscle of your thigh—here goes!' Soon after the injection, Sally's breathing relaxed and her normal colour returned. 'It will take a while for the blotches and welts on your body to disappear.'

Sally threw her arms around Belle. 'I'm so sorry for the trouble I've caused.'

Belle wasn't sure if the red flush in her face was sheer embarrassment or whether the toxin was still in her system.

By the time the ambulance arrived, Sally was out of danger but still had enough swelling and welts left to show it had been for real. She gave the paramedics a description of what had taken place and they commended Belle for her quick and competent action.

Dr Barlett was out of the area delivering a baby, so he would not have got there in time.

Belle felt useful at last. My extensive nursing career has not been in vain.

Sally recovered well and made sure she would warn others that she was allergic to bee stings in the future. She enjoyed the rest of her stay and said she would return again next year and would make a point of heeding the sign on the gate that reads....

Guests - Please Keep Out Of Orchard

****

The next morning, Belle heard Nancy shouting, 'Come back here you rascal—wait till I catch you!' The frenzied woman raced around the grass patch where the free-range hens roamed, trying to catch Charlie who was about to grab a chook. She managed to grab him by his collar and scold him severely. By the innocent expression on his face, he had no idea why she had admonished him. Embarrassed, Nancy took him back to the lodge bumping into Milton on the way.

'I'm so sorry Milton, I had no idea he had pulled off his lead. I thought he was still tied to the fence where I put him while I had afternoon tea.'

No problem—I've fixed up a run for him out back where he can tear around in a sheep pen. There's no stock there at present, and he can't get through the fence, so you can relax when he's outside. It's under that large oak tree.'

'Thanks so much—I was beginning to get stressed out— afraid he will hurt one of your hens or put them off laying. You're very kind.'

'Well, we can't have you packing up and leaving us already— especially when you were just beginning to relax and reap the benefits of Peace Haven. Don't you worry about Charlie, he'll be okay now.'

That's how it was with Milton and Belle, always going out of their way to make others feel at home and supported.

Belle liked to sit under the willows on one of the park benches and meditate. She relished the tranquillity, and during these times she would reminisce on how difficult and complicated her life used to be compared to how it was then.

She often reflected on how often her prayers were answered, and the grace of God—how he had granted her heart's desire in so many ways.

****

Belle's father Henry lived nearby in a rest-home, near Cromwell Mead where he had lived for a year after a bad fall, fracturing his pelvis. After he mended, Belle and Milton picked him up each Sunday and brought him home for a traditional roast which he eagerly anticipated. He would have liked to live with them, but the staff at the rest-home felt he would have been too difficult to manage due to his frailty. During the night he often became disorientated finding his way back to bed from the bathroom. There were other challenges too.

Henry loved to sit reminiscing with Belle on the veranda watching the sun go down. One evening, he took hold of Belle's hand and looked her in the eye. 'Belle—I want you to know something before it's too late for me to make amends.'

Belle wrinkled her brow, anxious about what would come next. 'What are you trying to say, Dad?'

'I'm so sorry about what I put you through when you were a youngster and all the confusion I caused. Your mother and I should have been truthful with you about your real paternity.'

Belle compulsively jumped in to rescue him from his guilt.

'Don't worry—I understand times were difficult then, and it would have caused such a scandal.'

'I know, but we went about it the wrong way putting Bernie's name on your Birth Certificate and all that.'

Henry broke down crying, holding his face in his hands.

'Dad, it's in the past—you mustn't be bogged down with guilt over it. I'm a survivor and learnt to live by my own wits somehow.' She squeezed his hand and offered to pray with him.

'If that's what you want I'll do it. Can you give me the words to say?' As they prayed, large teardrops rolled down his lined face as a broad smile broke out on his face. His jaw relaxed, and he suddenly appeared different to Belle, as though he'd been set free from all his guilt and shame.

****

A week after Henry's confession, the hospital phoned and Milton answered. 'Belle, it's the hospital on the phone. They said you had better come in now, Henry has taken a turn for the worst.'

When Belle arrived at the hospital Ward, her father was already in a coma and his breathing was laboured. The doctor said her father had suffered another fall hitting his head badly and fracturing his vertebrae.

'Hi Paul, I hope I'm not too late.' Belle said to the nurse. 'I'm going to stay with him tonight—is that okay?'

'Sure, of course—I'll arrange a recliner chair and blanket for you.' The nurse gave him some more morphine.

'Thanks very much. I'd hate to go home and have him pass away when I could have been with him.'

Belle found it hard to accept that she wasn't going to have her father around anymore, especially to catch up on all the lost time. She was going to be abandoned all over again.

Paul could see the sadness in Belle's face. 'You can talk to him. The last thing to leave a person is their hearing—he knows you are here.'

When Paul left the room, Belle sat next to the bed holding Henry's hand. She remembered the song that he always sang to her when she was a child. They used to sing it together—

'I'm on the road, on the road to anywhere

With never a heart-ache, with never a care.

Got no home, got no friends,

grateful for everything the good Lord sends.

On the road, on the road to anywhere,

Where every milestone seems to say

That with all the wear and care, the road to anywhere,

Will lead to somewhere, someday.'

Belle was sure she saw a faint smile appear on her father's lips and she felt a definite squeeze of her hand.

Milton was waiting in the lounge for her and poked his head through the door. 'Belle, I'll go home and get you some toiletries and clean clothes if you're going to stay the night. I'll be back soon.'

'That would be great if you could do that. Would you mind checking the bookings and make sure everyone is catered for? Cookie may need a hand in the morning too.'

'I'll ask Molly and Jock next door if they could give a hand with the animals tomorrow—I don't think you'll be back on deck by then.' Milton hurried out the door.

Paul, the nurse walked back in the room carrying a small, metal tray.

'Sorry, but I need to give Henry more pain relief. The morphine here will make him more comfortable.'

Belle stood aside.

'He's beginning to weaken, and I'm afraid I don't think he will see the night out,' he said with a soft voice.

With that, Belle was even more resigned to stay by his side until the end. She couldn't sleep—instead, she just sat staring at Henry's face for what seemed hours, hoping for signs of some kind of divine rejuvenation, imagining him sitting upright and coming alive again.

Henry let out a haunting sigh as if to gasp for his last breath, then it all went quiet in the room. Belle rang the bell for the nurse who arrived immediately and examined him.

Paul placed his hand on her shoulder. 'He has gone I'm afraid. I didn't think he would hold out as long as he did. You stay with him as long as you like—I'll call the doctor who has to sign his death certificate and get the staff to make you a cup of tea.'

Paul collected the recording charts hanging from Henry's bed while Belle mopped the tears that rolled down her cheeks.

She managed to force out words that were reluctant to have a voice. 'I appreciate that, thank you. I'll have to call my family.'

****

A short time after the funeral, Belle sat thinking about the unfairness of life. It seemed like a sick joke that Henry had entered her life after so many years then suddenly disappeared—especially before they had much quality time together. I've been robbed again. She used her sleeve this time to catch the avalanche that poured from tired eyes before she discovered a paper-towel holder on the wall.

Henry's passing left a gaping hole in Belle's life as a strong bond had developed between after his wife had died.

She spent days sitting on a seat next to the lake staring into the water and recalling all the good times they had shared during her youth.

Belle took his death hard. Peace Haven stayed closed for three weeks after Henry died, but it took Belle a long time to get used to life without him, however short their reunion had been.

****

Christmas and New Year came and went quickly that year and six months later, after a hectic summer season at the lodge, the weather cooled considerably. Everyone raced around preparing for Cromwell Mead's mid-winter Christmas dinner and barn dance held at the local community hall.

Milton and Murray stood on ladders erecting coloured lights around the hall and stringing magical fairy lights in the fir trees outside.

Belle and Annie were flat out baking pies, cup-cakes and sausage rolls while the locals brought their favourite dishes.

Harry and Jimmy managed to get away for a weekend with their wives to man the bar and operate the lamb-on-spit donated by Murray.

One of Milton's friends played saxophone in a small swing band who agreed to support the community event by providing dance music all evening. They were popular musicians, so this went down well.

'Milton—look over there—isn't it just sweet to see Murray and Annie dancing—they look so happy together.'

'I know—it's quite surprising, really. I was worried that Murray had shut himself down completely, so maybe a little romance is what he needs to pull him out of the doldrums.'

Belle handed Milton a glass of fruit punch. 'Well, I think he is really quite taken with our Annie.'

'They have both been to hell and back, although Murray is still in the thick of it. I suppose they can relate to one another.'

Belle had noticed that Murray was beginning to lose the strained look that she'd seen when they'd first met. She remembered the weathered face with deep furrows in his brow, weary and stressed looking. Now he could smile, and he had a spring in his step.

Belle remembered what a pale, lethargic woman Annie was when she first met her and how aged she'd appeared. Now she looked energised with pink cheeks and a pretty mop of shiny, auburn hair—signs of the noticeable effect that Peace Haven community had on her friend.

Later that day, there was a phone call from an old nursing colleague in Auckland who wanted to bring a friend to stay at the lodge.

'Hi, Josie—good to hear from you. How long will you both be staying, and who is your friend?'

'Corine is from Littleton in Wellington where she was working with the Salvation Army and I was introduced to her at a conference in Auckland. We thought we would stay for a week if that suits.'

'What is she doing in Auckland?'

'She was in need of a break and I heard she was looking for accommodation. I've had her boarding with me for a month now.'

Belle felt wary about her friend, a vulnerable widow, trusting a perfect stranger in her home. 'Well, you take care driving and have a safe journey. We'll expect you tomorrow afternoon.'

Belle wondered why Josie's daughter, Leah didn't have reservations about her mother taking in a complete stranger, knowing that Josie had recently become widowed.

She went out to their extensive veggie garden where she had a healthy flourishing herb plot that Cookie, took advantage of daily. She picked some Rosemary for her infamous Rosemary Sourdough bread, and Dill for an exotic fish dish.

Milton was busy checking the ponies' hooves to see which ones needed attention, prior to the Blacksmith's visit the next day. Belle had initially planned to breed foals and sell them as yearlings or two-year-olds. When the time came, it broke her heart the thought of seeing the youngsters ripped away from their mothers, as the ponies shared a close maternal bond with their foals.

She decided to keep them as pets and they were a great hit with the guests as well as the locals.

****

The next day, Josie arrived with her friend, Corine, who drove an old Mercedes Benz.

'Josie, it's so good to see you, it's been so long. You are looking pretty good … and you must be Corine—I've heard all about you.'

Corine shook hands with Belle and Milton. 'Only good things, I hope.' She gave them a sheepish grin.

Belle invited them into the lounge for high tea, while Milton took their luggage up to their rooms. They enjoyed the homebaked blueberry muffins together with Earl Grey tea Belle presented on a tea trolley.

Milton returned to join them. 'I hope you can get out and enjoy the sunshine, Josie. The weather is stable now, and I'm sure you'll enjoy the new English country garden we've made. We've made a new boardwalk through the garden to the lake.'

Before dinner that evening, Belle took Josie for a wander through the garden on the wooden boardwalk, while Corine, tired from driving, took a long nap. They meandered along the pathway to the lake then Belle invited Josie to sit with her on the aged wooden park bench. Two blue and purple butterflies, fluorescent in the sunlight, fluttered around their heads until they found the right bushes to settle on. One stopped on Belle's shoulder for an instant.

'Belle—I thought you might like to know I'm going overseas for three months.'

'Oh really—when will that be?'

'In August, while it is freezing cold here, I'll be enjoying the European Summer. Corine is taking me to lovely tourist spots such as Italy, Greece, Croatia and many other exotic places—even Spain and Morocco. The rest I can't remember.'

Belle frowned, concerned at Josie's welfare, knowing the woman was well into her seventies and not robust in health.

'Well, that's radical—it'll be exhausting if you are flying everywhere.'

'No, we're taking a world cruise and only fly to London to meet the ship there.'

'Sounds idyllic—I'll bet that's setting you back a dollar or two—if you don't mind me saying.'

'My husband, Gerald left me a substantial sum with his life insurance which I invested on a term deposit. It has returned good interest, so I decided I can't take it with me to the grave—I may as well enjoy it now.'

Belle wondered how Corine could afford to go too if she only worked at the Salvation Army as a volunteer. And the fact that she organised the whole trip herself, concerned Belle.

Later that evening at dinner, Belle felt uneasy around Corine. There was something about her that just didn't add up, as she didn't let Josie out of her sight and appeared to control her every move. She also seemed to scrutinise everyone at the dinner table, as though she was scheming something. Was this elder abuse? Belle wondered.

Milton began to quiz her. 'Corine—what brings you to Wellington? I hear you have been working with the Salvation Army down there?'

'I've been working with homeless people in Littleton which is exhausting work and I need a break. I'm hoping to find something less demanding now that I'm semi-retired.'

Belle wanted to pry more information out of Corine with Josie and Milton as witnesses, but there were other guests at the end of the table.

'And you are both off to Europe, Josie mentioned. That must cost a small fortune, all those countries you are going to be visiting for three months. Josie showed us the travel brochures.'

'Oh yes, that's right. An aunt left me a small fortune, so I can now start travelling. I've wanted to do this trip for years and now I can.'

Milton looked sideways at Belle. They both went into the kitchen to make coffee.

Belle whispered, 'That seems so suspect that she has inherited a fortune just when she is about to take Josie off on a world trip. I don't like the sound of this at all Milton.'

'We can't make assumptions when we've only just met her. Just see how things go while they are staying here, and if you're still worried after they return home, you could give Leah a ring and express your concerns to her.'

They both brought the coffee and cake to the dining table joined the guests again. The two foreign couples who were guests for the weekend had excused themselves and gone off to bed, tired out from their trip to the Kaimai Ranges earlier that day.

Corine took a second cup of coffee and Josie drank a cup of herb tea while they sat for an hour chatting with Belle and Milton.

Belle gazed at Corine's eyes. There was something odd about their colour and she couldn't pinpoint what the problem was. The woman's heavily dyed blonde hair appeared unnatural—it didn't fit her face. There was just something not right about her appearance.

Milton and Belle hinted they were off to bed and the two women took themselves to their rooms.

Milton checked that all the doors were locked, turned off the lights and retreated to their master bedroom with Belle in tow. She chatted to him while he was in the ensuite cleaning his teeth.

'I find it hard to believe that Corine is from the Salvation Army, as she appears so fake—not the type for that calling. Perhaps I should phone Leah after the women return to Auckland.'

<h1 style="text-align:center">Chapter Seven</h1>

After the two women returned home, Belle heard nothing from Josie and phoned Leah to express her concerns about the possibility of Corine being a con artist. She said she would check it out and get back to her.

A month later during a trip to Auckland, Belle bumped into a mutual friend of Josie's.

'Have you heard from Josie? She brought a friend down to stay at Peace Haven recently, and since she went back to Auckland, we have heard nothing from her.'

'Didn't you know—something awful has happened to her?'

'What do you mean—is she ill or something? I hope not.'

Belle gazed hard at the woman who seemed reluctant to discuss it and became agitated.

'No, not that bad, but a con-artist—a woman who claimed to have worked for the Salvation Army cheated her out of thousands!'

'You mean a woman called Corine?'

'I think that's her name. Anyway, my Mum told me that this woman had been boarding with Josie and offered to take her to Europe. She defrauded her of ten thousand dollars which she took as a down payment for the trip and deposited it into her own bank account. The next morning, she packed up and left Josie high and dry.'

'I knew something wasn't right with that woman—I didn't trust her from the start when she arrived to stay with us, and I rang her daughter to say I felt uneasy about her.'

'Mum knows her daughter, Leah too,' said her friend.

'She said the police apprehended her at the airport, just in time. Apparently, she has a police record for serial fraud. She uses coloured contact lenses and dies her black hair blond. She even uses different aliases, so poor Josie didn't stand a chance.'

'Oh, poor Josie—she must be so shaken up—she was so vulnerable and lonely. We'll have to get her down to stay with us again until she recovers. I'll talk to Milton about it tonight.'

'Well, I'm sorry to have to break the bad news to you,' said her friend. 'I must get on now—take care.'

Belle felt sad for Josie, as she had been through a rough time the last few years, and who would have thought that she would be conned into taking a fraudster into her home? Though it could have been worse—she could have robbed her once they were in Europe and abandoned her, leaving her stranded, I guess.

A few months later, Belle received more bad news about Josie when Belle and Milton had organised for her to visit them again. She planned to attend a weekend Women's Conference with ladies from her church and then travel to Peace Haven with her friend Irene afterwards.

Leah rang Belle to say there had been a terrible accident. And both women had died in a head-on collision—killed outright. Belle's legs crumbled at the news when she hung the phone up. Why is it that such bad things happen to such good people?

She sat by the fireplace staring into the glow, pondering the fragility of life and how easily we can take people for granted.

****

Belle wandered through their rambling English garden by the hen-house and caught sight of Milton waving at her on the veranda. 'Belle, it's Rose—she's got some good news for you.'

She rushed to the phone.

'Mum, I'm pregnant! I never thought it was going to happen and had given up. I've been nauseated for weeks and those funny changes have started happening with my body.'

'Belle, that's fantastic—it's an answer to prayer! I just knew if you stopped trying so hard, it would happen when you least expected it.'

'I know Mum, it's so amazing. I had a scan and I'm nearly three months on now. Mum—I wanted to ask you if you could do me a favour? If Milton could spare you for a short time, I'd like you to be with me at the birth, and after I go home for a few weeks.'

'Of course, I can be with you—I'll look forward to it and I'm sure Milton would want that too. I'll talk to him today.'

'What about your guests and animals?'

'We have a lovely couple who have given us relief in the past. If they can help out, we can both come. They are retired motel managers, and more recently, missionaries. Milton could help Andy with lambing and I could ask Murray from next door to watch over our animals. Annie might help with feeding the hens.'

'Thanks, Mum, I'll leave it up to you, but let's see how it all goes first. Just pray my pregnancy goes well.'

Milton was thrilled with the news too. They were both looking forward to more grandchildren.

****

Three months later, Rose had some more surprising news. 'Mum, I'm having twins! I didn't know there were twins in the family, are there?'

'I told you my father was a twin. But it can just happen, anyway. I'm not sure about the biology of twins, I can't remember my science lessons and how it all works. Milton and I will come and stay with you a few days before you go into hospital.'

Belle was so excited she found it hard to concentrate on the task ahead at Peace Haven for the next few months.

The cold months were drawing to an end and Belle longed for the first signs of spring to appear. In spite of the wintery weather, Peace Haven had remained full most of the time.

One night, Belle, who had acute hearing, woke with a start when she heard a loud rumble.

'Milton, wake up!'

'What is it Belle—I was sound asleep?'

She grabbed his arm. 'The ground is moving, and the bed is swaying!'

'Oh, no—we should get under the door post if it gets any stronger'. Milton wrapped his arm around her to reassure her.

'I hope Annie is alright. During that bad earthquake last year she lost her home and husband. Now she suffers from post-traumatic stress and is still recovering.'

'You had better pop along to her room and make sure she is okay. I'll come and wait outside the door.'

'I'll see if her light is on, and if it is, I'll ask if she wants to come down to the lounge for a cuppa.'

A sudden jolt and more shaking unnerved Belle as they walked along the hallway to Annie's room whose light was on as she knocked on the door. When Annie opened it, she looked as though she'd seen a ghost.

'Are you okay, Annie—you felt the jolt too, eh? Milton and I thought you might like to stay with us for a while, until the shaking stops. We may have to crawl under the dining room table if it gets worse.'

****

The news was grim. A substantial earthquake had flattened a small town on the East Coast, but not as severe as the one that Annie had experienced when she lost her husband. The Civil Defence was still busy evacuating victims and transferring them to a community hall where the Salvation Army and Red Cross fed them and handed out blankets.

During the rest of the day, there were continual news updates on the radio and by the evening, when Belle and Milton watched the news on television, there had been no reported deaths but many people were hospitalised. Only minor aftershocks were felt in Cromwell Mead.

Belle lay snuggled up next to Milton in front of their wood burner resting her head on his shoulder thinking about Annie to whom they offered a room close to their flat.

Milton turned to look at Belle. 'You've gone unusually quiet this evening. Is everything alright?'

'I can't stop feeling sorry for Annie. She not only lost her home and husband in the earthquake down south a few years ago, but I think she also lost herself and relived it all over again last night. Her son who lives near Winton Abbot often works overseas and is due to return home at the end of the year to start building a flat on his property for her. Until then, she'll have to find a home to rent as his place is too small as it is. She can't live forever in one of our rooms.'

'It's strange you should say that as I've been thinking about what to do with the cottage, now that our tenants have gone.'

Milton put another log on the fire and sat down. He continued, 'After we saw what state Annie was in last night, and you'd told me she'd been to hell and back, I had an idea. What about offering her the cottage for a token rent—at least until she gets on her feet or until her son comes back at the end of the year?'

Belle appeared elated. 'That's a wonderful thought and a great idea. Funny you say that, as I've been thinking along those lines too. It must be claustrophobic living out of an ensuite bedroom long term.'

'Well, why don't you go along and tell her about our idea and see if it suits her?'

Belle found Annie in her room looking at photos of her family and overwhelmed at Belle's proposal overwhelmed her. The floodgates opened as she began to sob. 'You've no idea how worried I've been. My nerves have been bad since the earthquake when I lost my home and I haven't been able to afford anything to rent in Winton Abbot and it'll be months before I receive the payout from the insurance company for my house.'

'I'm so pleased that we can ease your burden, Annie, as we've been quite concerned. Any other way we can help, just let us know.'

Annie produced a broad smile. 'I appreciate your kindness, thanks so much.'

'You can make arrangements to move into the cottage any time now. I hope you won't mind the chickens wandering around, as they can make a bit of a mess, but the droppings are good for the gardens.'

'It makes me feel at home, as I had free-range chickens too—anyway, they already know me when I feed them and collect their eggs.'

Belle wandered back to the homestead after showing Annie around the cottage. She came to the realisation that the vision of helping the lonely, lost and broken-hearted had come to fruition and had been unfolding ever since she married Milton.

Chapter Eight

A month later spring arrived. Belle felt a sense of excited expectancy, as though good things were in store.

It was time for her and Milton to pack up and go to the high country so that they could be with Rose in preparation for her elective Caesarean Section and birth of her twins. Belle was eager to see her daughter and Milton looked forward to a break from Peace Haven to help Andy with the ewes which were about to start lambing.

The small aircraft landed at Queenstown Airport where they were met by Andy who drove them for an hour along precipitous, dirt roads to Perrendale.

Milton and Belle absorbed the amazing views, as the four-wheel drive headed up the steep hills. They could see for miles on such a clear day, and the fields were still green. During the middle of summer, the fields turned brown and were often plagued by drought.

As they arrived at the large homestead, Rose stood by the door beaming, noticeably pregnant. The poor girl could hardly walk. Belle was relieved there was a highly reputable birthing unit near Wanaka.

The farm cook had prepared a wholesome traditional meal and the delicious aroma of lamb stew wafted down the hallway.

Rose offered her parents the guest room with extensive views from the veranda where they discovered a wooden bench they could relax on in the evenings as the sun went down.

****

The next morning, Belle helped Rose sort out the room for the twins. She'd brought gifts for them—mainly baby nursery supplies to keep her going for a while.

When it was time for Rose to go to the birthing unit, they all accompanied her. Belle and Milton spent the day there until the babies were born, and Andy stayed with Rose the whole time. The twins arrived safcly in perfect health and screaming for a feed. They named them Fleur and Pierre, a girl and boy—the perfect package—a gift from God.

Belle kept going from the crack of dawn and crashed into bed late at night, supporting her daughter every way she could while she struggled to carry two babies in her arms with a belly full of stitches. She was very sore and tired, but at least she had plenty of milk, for these were large babies.

Milton was in his element as he reminisced about his own childhood on the farm. There was so much work to be done, and although Andy had several station hands, a few of them were away on leave, so Milton's assistance came at the right time. They either went on horse-back or rode quad bikes, depending on how steep the land was. After the evening meal, Milton found it hard to stay awake after working so hard on the station each day. He and Belle both went to bed early each evening.

By the time they were ready to set off back to Peace Haven, Rose's house-keeper had returned from her break and Andy's station hands had arrived back that day, so they didn't have to cope on their own.

Rose and Andy assured Belle that they would bring the babies to Peace Haven for Christmas, as they would be able to travel by then.

Belle hated to leave Rose to cope without her, but she knew her to be a strong and capable girl, and if she really needed her, her mother would be straight down there. Belle found the house-keeper to be a reliable woman—a trained nurse who had a good reputation with children.

****

When they arrived back at Peace Haven, it was, to their surprise, completely full. It was obvious to them that their friends Molly and Jock, who had managed Peace Haven for them, were in their element. They chatted away to everyone at the dinner table, keeping them involved.

Annie had moved into the cottage already and entertained herself feeding the hens while Belle and Milton were away. She was very much at home there, and Molly and Jock had kept a close eye on her to see that she was safe in the cottage.

Later that day, Milton had a visit from Murray and they appeared to be having a serious talk on the veranda, which Belle had observed as she wandered back from the lake. Murray stayed for afternoon tea and he was pleased his friend had returned from down south.

'I have half a side of lamb for you again if you'd like one.'

'Great', said Milton. 'We're getting low on meat and we haven't had time to do a big shop in Winton Abbot with the twins arriving.'

'Wonderful—you can fix me up at the end of the month if you like. I'd like some of your free-range eggs though if you can spare them.'

Milton handed Murray a cold beer and sat down on the stone wall next to him. He squinted, glaring at the deep craters under his eyes.

'I think there's something you want to talk to me about—you appear to be troubled.'

'I've been getting hassled by that new American crowd of money-grabbing cheats from that stinking Zenith property outfit.'

'What are they up to now? I hear they've been pressuring folk to sell their land to them. They are the same lot that owns that huge Country Club Resort in Texas, the one that attracts celebrities.'

'Well we don't want them here—they're out to ruin the heritage of generations of owners of cherished family farming estates here.'

'So, in what way have they been harassing you, Murray?'

'There is this bloke who calls himself Peta Arnott, a right "yes man" for Mike Bowman the owner of Zenith Corporation. He phoned me a couple of times last month trying to persuade me to sell my land to them.'

'Why would he phone you out of the blue?'

'He said he'd heard I'd lost interest in my farm since my wife died and had been thinking of selling my dairy herd and business.'

'Is that right? I thought you loved being on the farm, and I haven't seen any signs of you losing interest.'

'I may have told a mate or two I was finding things a bit difficult since Lily died and was thinking of giving up the milking. I never said I was selling the farm.'

'What happened then? Did he accept your answer or are they still harassing you? You know you can pull in the big guns if they don't leave you alone.'

'That big fella, Peta Arnott came to the house two days ago and literally started looking around my property uninvited with a clipboard and camera.'

'He can't do that on private property!' Milton erupted.

'I asked him to leave, and he gave me some phoney story that he thought I had organised a visit with someone from the Corporation but must have got it wrong.'

'Con artist!' said Milton, fuming. He topped up Murry's glass with cold Heineken and could see he looked stressed.

'He drove away with a sinister look on his face, creepy sort of and I don't trust them—they are up to no good. I know they are desperate for my land, especially as it has a lake with salmon. It's a perfect spot for a country club resort and casino. I've had a few incidences with my animals being randomly slaughtered—a few cows and three sheep were killed mercilessly a few months ago.' Murray's voice shook slightly as he was becoming emotionally distraught.

'Let me know if you get any more of those phone calls or strange visits, as I've got a friend who works for the local police and will speak to him. I also know people who handle resource consents for the use of rural land. They would be very interested to hear about these dirty tactics he uses to take ownership of good agricultural land.'

'That's good of you Milton, but I'm sure you have enough to do with running your own farmlet, and the lodge keeps you busy. A guest house can be demanding.'

'Perhaps it's time for you to have some time out again and come and stay with us for a week or two. You still have Joe, your farmhand with you and I'm sure he can manage while you're away. At least you won't be there if they come knocking.'

Belle called the men onto the veranda for snacks she had prepared—Milton's favourite home-made sausage rolls, made from the side of beef that Murray had sold them a few months ago.

Murray hastily tucked into the hot savouries, dipping them into the bowl of homemade tomato sauce.

He winked at Milton. 'You certainly get well looked after, mate. Perhaps I'll consider your offer after all.'

Chapter Nine

Three days later, as Milton sat on his ride-on mower by the lake, billows of dark smoke above the trees bordering Murray's farm caught his attention. He motored full throttle back to the house shouting out to Belle that he was going over there to investigate, and to keep the radiophone handy.

Milton gathered it must have been Murray burning off green waste, although he usually waits until it is dried out. Suddenly angry flames erupted from one end of the barn.

In the distance, he could see Joe riding his quad-bike up on the ridge.

Meanwhile, Murray had found his way through the suffocating smoke to the window in the barn roof. He looked around the barn and his only way out was the roof, but the heat was rose rapidly into the roof space. He would have to go through the roof window. At least the fire was mostly at the other end of the barn.

He tried to muster the courage to jump—'God please give me the courage to jump,' he cried.

He plunged below, landing with an agonising thud as he twisted his leg on impact. He screamed as he clutched his leg then attempted to drag himself away and crawled like a lame dog as the smoke filled his lungs causing him to retch.

As Milton drove up towards the house, he wondered if Murray had spilt fuel in the barn and accidentally set it alight.

He rang the fire brigade then looked for him as he called out to frantically. He began to despair he may have been too late as he was nowhere in the house to be found.

'Can you hear me, Murray?

Milton thought he could hear a man's voice near the barn. As he raced around the back, the building started collapsing and through the haze of smoke, he saw the silhouette of a man dragging himself away from the inferno.

Racing towards him he shouted, 'Murray, is that you? Thank God it is—let me help you!'

'I can't walk—I broke my leg jumping out of the barn window— it was my only way out. Some mongrel deliberately locked me in and set it alight. I heard them driving off.'

Murray clutched Milton's sleeve. 'Quickly—drag me over there in case there's an explosion. My quad bike and tractor are inside full of fuel.'

Milton grabbed him under his arms, which was no easy feat, and dragged him to safety.

'I'm ringing the ambulance and police. Where do you keep your pain-killers inside the house?'

'In the medicine cabinet in the bathroom—I'm dehydrated too.'

His face looked like a chimney sweep and his singed hair had balded him. Milton barely recognised him. 'I'll bring you some water.'

The ambulance arrived quickly. The paramedics assessed the patient then raced him off to the hospital. The police officer had told him he would be questioned once he was stable in hospital. They also wanted to question Joe who had just arrived at the scene. He was left to milk the cows and Milton offered to help out if necessary.

Someone deliberately tried to kill Murray. After the detectives searched the property for clues, they suspected the owners of Zenith Corporation, but the police needed to find clear evidence.

One of the detectives found a gold neck chain amongst the charred remains of the barn with the initials P. A engraved under a disc hanging on a chain.

Joe, a key witness, made a statement for the police. He had seen someone arriving at Murray's property immediately before the fire when he was on his way back to the barn after rescuing a sheep that had fallen into a ditch. As he approached Murray's homestead, he could see in the distance a black Ute travelling along the private road to the farm. It entered the property and parked further back from the house, under a cluster of trees, waiting there for a short time then raced off. Joe saw the smoke coming from the property, thinking Murry must have been burning rubbish.

****

When Murray was discharged from hospital with his leg in plaster, Milton and Belle offered to take him to convalescence until he could get back on his feet.

They helped him sort out the insurance claim for the fire and learned that he would be able to get a completely new barn built.

He made the most of Belle and Milton pampering him, and the hearty homecooked meals. At their long, French rustic dining table, he relished sitting next to Annie when she came for a lamb roast once a week, as Belle thought she could do with socialising a bit more.

Gregarious Annie delighted in chatting away to the guests and most of all fraternising with Murray.

During Murray's stay at Peace Haven, the police arrested Peta Arnott who already had a criminal record in America for attempted murder and arson, and Mike Bowman as an accessory. Both were given a prison sentence.

84

The Zenith Corporation was forbidden to operate in New Zealand, and the rest of the shareholders returned to America. At last, the people of Cromwell Mead were free of the thugs and could get back to living normal lives.

It was time for Murray to head back to his own farm, and with his leg out of plaster, he felt safe to return home.

Belle, Milton, and especially Annie kept a close eye on him along with a few neighbours who know him well.

****

A few months later, Murray climbed over the wooden gate to tell Milton and Belle eager to tell he'd sold his farm.

'I've made some massive changes over there at Ferndale. I've sold the farm to my neighbour—one hundred-and-ninety acres, and retained twenty acres including the house which I may turn into an orchard. The soil quality is the right kind, apparently. When I retire, I can sell off the rest of the land to him as he said he wants the first option.'

Milton wilted at the thought of his friend leaving.

'Where will you live now?'

'He and his wife have bought my farm labourers' cottage on the back of my farm, and I'll stay living in my homestead for the time being, until I decide what to do with the twenty acres.'

Milton looked at Murray with bewilderment and relief.

85

'Wow, that's pretty radical, but I understand you need to do this.'

'Well, that way, I don't have all the work to do, and can enjoy waking in the morning to my mates, the cows looking over the fence at me, still feeling at home.'

'Well, I think it's an ingenious idea, Murray.' Milton chuckled. 'I can imagine you staring into the faces of cows each morning—the ones with the long eyelashes and dreamy faces.'

'The new owners are not going to be milking—they want to fatten beef, as the prices are pretty good at present and the future looks better with fat cattle.'

'It's a win-win plan for all of you. Good thing you have two homes on the land. What do you think you'll grow on the twenty acres?'

'I've heard that blueberries fetch a high price, especially if grown organically. I'll plant a few acres of those and put the rest in seedless mandarin trees. There's a great demand for them now on the local market and I'll keep sheep on the surplus.'

'Sounds like a good plan to me.'

'And you'll still get your side of lamb now and then.' Murray said winking at Milton as he turned to wander back home.

Milton arrived to find Belle sitting on the veranda looking downcast. She quizzed him about the serious talk he had with

Murry, as she noticed his intense mood. After Milton had told her the news, she was disappointed.

'I don't think he ever expected anything like that would happen to him. I mean who would? Lily died a slow, lingering death that left him bereaved and debilitated for years—now this! Life seems so unfair at times!'

Milton looked lovingly at Belle. 'That's true. But you have heard—the rain falls on the good and bad alike. Nobody is exempt from misfortune, Belle, and no one knows that better than you.'

<h1 style="text-align:center">Chapter Ten</h1>

Milton took Belle's hand as they wandered back inside the lounge. She snuggled up to him on the couch.

'I have a feeling Murray doesn't really want to lose us as neighbours, and he values our friendship. It's good that Belle.'

He affectionately put his arm around her waist.

'It funny that, because I feel the same about Annie. She seems reluctant to move on too, as though she wants to settle down here.'

The next morning, Belle rose early and picked fresh flowers from her English country garden that contained every flower imaginable. She placed them in quaint little vases for the dining table.

'Belle, are you near the office— you get the phone, please? I have dirty boots!' Milton bellowed.

It was Rose on the phone. 'Hi, Mum—did you see the photos of the twins I sent you? The large photo is on the front page of our local rag.'

'Yes, we did, Rose— they are so cute in the Pumpkin Patch clothes I sent them. I didn't think they would fit them for another month or two—they've grown so much.'

'We'll be there at Christmas, all goes well. It will be a busy time for you all, Mum.'

Belle couldn't wait for that day, no matter how busy it would be.

****

Christmas was always a hectic time at Peace Haven, although it was not open to guests for three weeks while the family were there. They invited Murray who was grateful for the company and Annie who still lived in the cottage.

This was a joyful time for Belle—especially the family times picnicking by the lagoon which was a tradition each year. The meadows were covered with wildflowers and azure blue butterflies during summer—her little piece of paradise.

Max couldn't wait to get amongst the horses. No sooner had he arrived, he took the grooming gear from the saddlery shed and after brushing the animal hastily, he went riding on his favourite pony, Horace, while Belle accompanied him on her own horse, Valour.

As usual, Belle sat next to Milton in the evening, watching the pastel pink sunset change as the sun went down. She was tired after entertaining the family.

'Isn't that Murray over there by the lake walking with someone? Looks like he is with Annie,' she said pointing in their direction.

'Yes, I've noticed how chummy they are when I saw them yesterday after breakfast. Annie showed him her new garden and the landscaping she has done.'

Belle poured Milton and herself a glass of fresh-squeezed lemonade. 'It's good to see them enjoying themselves. They both need it for sure.'

Since Annie had moved to the cottage, she and Murray had been grown closer, going for afternoon walks around the lake, and even going to the odd country dance, now that Murray's leg had healed.

Belle and Milton could see the healing taking place in their lives, as they began to be happy again. This evening, they observed Murray taking Annie on a guided tour of the farm, as they walked back arm in arm.

'I don't think we are going to see Annie going to live in Winton Abbot now. I think she has settled in for good,' said Belle, observing a true romance blooming.

'We could ask Murray if he'd like to manage our lawns on the ride-on mower, seeing that Albert is leaving us at the end of the month.' Milton Replied.

'I think Annie is interested in giving us a hand to run the retreat. She has offered to help in the kitchen and has good business skills, so could assist in the office too. It's her way of giving back a little.' Belle had made a good friend in Annie who had become like a sister to her.

'That sounds great, Belle. Perhaps we could start paying her once she knows the ropes.'

****

Murray planted fruit trees and berry crops in his new orchard with the help of Joe whom he kept on, and agreed to mow the lawns at Peace Haven for a fee on a regular basis. Whenever he finished the lawns on the ride-on mower, Annie rushed to his side with a freshly baked chicken or his favourite lasagne. She watched him from a distance like a stalker and Belle guessed she showed signs of falling in love.

In return, Murray gave Annie succulent blueberries straight from his own bushes in the hope she would make him a blueberry pie to put with cream from his neighbour.

Peace Haven became a refuge for the lonely, lost and broken-hearted. It was a real manifestation of the vision Belle had carried for years.

91

All around her in Cromwell Mead there appeared to be the walking wounded. Belle knew that life was very fragile, and it was easy to take one's health or good fortune in life for granted. A tragedy could be lurking just around the next corner.

She was grateful that she had a strong faith in God, and fear did not control her life as it did many others.

She and her husband, as hosts at Peace Haven, did not push their spiritual beliefs on others, though they were open to discussion and spiritual guidance if a guest showed interest.

They were both trained in grief counselling and put their skills to much use at Peace Haven.

Many of their guests were referred for rehabilitation by their Health Providers and received a government subsidy, while others were private paying guests or tourists as the lodge was open to everybody.

In the grounds at Peace Haven stool the little chapel—an octagonal red brick building covered in ivy, with stunning leadlight windows and the roof displayed an ornate glass skylight. It was popular with guests seeking quietness and meditation.

Pretty red and green parakeets flocked to the tall kowhai tree next to the chapel to feed off the nectar in the bright yellow flowers.

****

Farming in Cromwell Mead and throughout the country became tough as global milk prices dropped and huge droughts ravaged other parts of the country. Many farmers took their own lives and special counselling services were set up all around the country to assist the victims.

A few counsellors used Peace Haven facilities weekly to provide support—people who had specialised training in suicide prevention that was funded by the Rural Mental Health Services.

Near Peace Haven lived Belle's friend, Cherie Drew on Ambury Farm. She had met Cherie a few years earlier at the Women's Institute and she was now pregnant with her first child. Her husband, Tom was the son of a sheep farmer from the South.

One morning, Belle dropped by to visit Cherie with a blueberry pie and a small quilt she had made for the baby's bassinet.

'How have you been getting on Cherie—you are due soon aren't you?'

'Yes, I'm okay but just tired. It's the heat—not easy carrying this load in the peak of summer.'

'You must try to get your feet up more— honestly, it'll stop your legs aching and prevent the swelling.'

'There are too many jobs to do on the farm, and I can't leave everything to Tom as he's quite stressed right now, especially following that last drought. The sheep need vaccinating and drenching and there's a lot to do. Tom doesn't seem to be well for some reason.'

'Maybe he needs to see the local doctor for a routine check-up.'

'He won't do that. He doesn't trust doctors and tries to handle everything his own way.'

Belle tried to encourage her without seeming bossy. 'Nevertheless—you should try to get him to see reason, as running so much livestock is a big job, and he needs to be fit.'

****

Belle did not hear anything from Cherie for a few weeks after that visit and thought everything must have been alright—until she received a phone call from Cherie's mother who was staying with her.

'Hullo, is that Belle Spencer? I'm Cherie Drew's mother, Beth.'

'Hi Beth, is everything alright—how can I help?'

'Cherie asked me to phone to let you know something terrible has happened.' Beth's voice quavered. 'Tom has been killed in an accident—a shooting accident, we think.' She burst into tears again while Belle waited for her to compose herself.

'Gosh, that's dreadful, Beth. I'm so sorry—poor Cherie.'

'Yes, just as her baby is about to be born. I'll be staying on here until she goes into labour. Tom's family are handling the funeral and we'll keep you informed.'

'Please give my condolences to Cherie and tell her if there is anything we can do, please phone us.'

Beth hung the phone up before Belle could say any more.

She called out to Milton to share the terrible news.

'Milton, I need to talk to you. I've had some horrible, upsetting news.'

'Come and sit down for a while, Belle, I'll put the billy on first.' Milton carried a tray with tea in Belle's bone china teapot and started pouring.

'Tell me what's happened—you look as though you've seen a ghost.'

'It's poor Cherie's husband—he's been killed.'

'What—was it a car crash?'

'No, a shooting accident, Beth, her mother said. I only saw Cherie a couple of weeks ago. She more or less let on Tom was fairly stressed.'

'That's dreadful, poor girl. How did it happen?'

'Her mother didn't say. I'll pop up to see her, as she'd like to talk to me. I think her Mum is staying on for a month until after the funeral, which is this Sunday afternoon.'

Milton asked Annie if she could manage the bookings on the day of the funeral and asked Murray he if could drop by to make sure Annie was okay. Naturally, Murray didn't mind keeping an eye on her.

After Tom's funeral, Belle and Milton offered to support Cherie once her parents returned home, and her father, a conveyancing lawyer, handled the sale of the farm.

Belle invited Cherie to stay at Peace Haven with baby Ruby for as long as she wanted until her farm sold. Cherie burst into tears of gratitude, as she was concerned about her future with Ruby.

Her father returned to his law practice in Winton Abbot, and her mother stayed on for a while to help her get their affairs in order, prior to the sale of the property. The farmhand was able to manage the stock with the help of neighbours.

They sold Ambury Farm to a family from the East Coast who moved closer to their relatives.

Chapter Eleven

'Belle—Cherie just phoned. Can you ring her back? She wants to stay for a month, now that her mother has gone back home.'

Belle stood out on the veranda seeing guests off while Milton stayed on the phone chatting to Cherie offering her support. She looked forward to spending time with her friend before she left Cromwell Mead to live in Winton Abbot near her parents.

She flicked through the booking register. 'Milton—I think we need to limit the bookings while Cherie is with us, so we can both spend with her before she ventures out on her own again.'

'You're right—I guess she'll need plenty of emotional support right now.'

'This week, we just have the Croatian couple who were victims of the Lindt Chocolate café shootings. You know—the people who were hostages.'

'Oh yes, I remember. Annie asked me is she could take them on tours in our van around the coast, now she has her Passenger Licence. Murray offered to accompany her, which is good.'

****

Cherie arrived the next day appearing gaunt and pale with three-month-old Ruby.

Belle wrapped her arm around Cherie's waist. 'I know what you need, Cherie—some of my blueberry pie and my neighbour's fresh cream, straight from the cow.'

The neighbour she referred to was not Murray—it was Monty, who owned the dairy farm on the other side of Peace Haven called Winslow Farm.

Monty and his wife Beryl, a couple in their late sixties often dropped in with a billy can full of thick yellow cream, that is, the cream from the top of the milk—a real highlight for the guests, especially if Belle clotted it and served it with fresh strawberry jam on hot scones. Devonshire Teas were Belle's speciality.

This year, milk prices shot up globally, and dairy farmers did well, including Monty. He bartered with Milton while visiting and took home a bucket of Belle's fresh herbs and berries. They didn't have time for gardening as well as milking cows, he told them.

Cherie settled into her bedroom with Queen Bed and ensuite, admiring the English country style duvet covered in an array of red and pink flowers with shades of green. Belle had allotted her the Family Suite with an adjoining room with a cot for Ruby.

Through the French doors, she could see the lake in the distance, lined with willows and poplar trees.

Next to the veranda, the yellow kowhai tree was full of tuis and other native birds making a melodic commotion. A strong fragrance emanating from the rambling roses on the railing wafted through her door.

As Cherie looked about the room, colourful oil paintings caught her attention—especially the one with bright yellow, willowy cornfields which she found comforting, feeling at home in this special room.

The bonus for her was the modern ensuite with a deep spa bath, and a window with one-way glass, which looked out at the kowhai tree.

When she took a long-awaited soak in the bath, she saw that Belle had taken care of her by placing on the vanity, fancy organic beauty items for her to use—a large jar of lavender bath salts for aching muscles, a body scrub containing avocado oil, honey, almond milk and apricot kernels. On the washbasin stood a bottle of moisturiser with coconut milk and jojoba. An elegant bath towel with matching white flannel with red roses hung from the vanity cabinet. Everything smelled so good and fresh—Cherie felt cherished.

The warm bath made her sleepy, and she took a nap while Annie took baby Ruby for a walk around the lake in her pram, with her mother's consent.

An hour later Cherie awoke refreshed and energised. As she rose from the bed, she could see Belle through the glass picking roses next to the veranda.

She stood in the doorway with a lilac, merino shawl draped around her shoulders. 'Hi, Belle. Thanks so much for making my room so welcoming—those gorgeous coloured freesias next to the bed and all the lovely smellies in the ensuite. I really appreciate it.'

'Oh, Cherie—that's nothing. I like to spoil our guests who come here for a break, especially my friends.'

'I suppose I'd better go and rescue poor Annie. I hope Ruby has behaved.'

'I think you might have trouble pulling her away from our Annie—she is quite taken with her. Ruby slept in the pram, but I think she may be ready for another feed now.'

'What a relief—I hoped she wouldn't be any trouble while I'm staying here.'

'You have no fear of that, Cherie. Annie and I will take turns looking after her if you have no objections, and Milton loves babies too, so everything will be fine—don't worry.'

'That's kind of you—she seems to like you all.'

Cherie settled in well and resolved much of her grief while at Peace Haven. Belle and Milton advised her that it could take a few years to heal, and recommended participating in the programme, Restoring Past Foundations.

During her counselling session, she told her story;

'I found out soon after Tom's funeral when an autopsy was carried out, that Tom had committed suicide. It was so sad for his parents as he was their only child. After his death, his mother confessed to me that he had suffered from a psychological condition called Narcissistic Personality Disorder as a teenager. He went off the rails at that time, causing the family a great deal of stress. Tom's parents were so pleased when I married him— hoping I could straighten him out, as they believed he would grow out of it.

When I first met him at Waikato University, he was a real pretty boy, several years older than me. My parents didn't like him much, but they couldn't keep me away from him. He was a typical narcissistic manipulator who knew I came from a family with status and money, but I suppose his good looks were the magnate for me.

He came from a farming background, but during his youth, showed no interest in farming. When his father retired, they sold the farm, and he and his wife bought a smaller property in Taupo.

Tom met me at the university café at the university where I had casual work while studying there. He was doing his Agricultural degree part-time.

 After we married, he began to get a yearning for country life and wanted a fresh start and we both decided to make a good go of it. His parents retired to a small house and purchased Ambury Farm in Cromwell Mead as an investment for Tom, hoping it might encourage him and that gave us a good financial start. I invested money from the sale of my cottage in Winton Abbot into the farm.

During our difficult marriage, Tom was excessively controlling, often pushing me around if I didn't submit to his every whim and desire. He had taken some theology studies in the past and became obsessive, often spouting that a wife must be completely under her husband's rule. I bucked his insane regime—being an independent woman, as I knew it was unhealthy as he was sadistic and selfish.

I was afraid to leave him for fear of losing face with my family and friends—and my church was against divorce so I felt trapped. I journaled all the events of the abuse, especially the life-threatening ones and documented records

One summer, Tom took me along to one of his so-called favourite spots at the beach at Lang's Cove. He took me up the path that went around the cliff face onto a tight, narrow goat

track covered with slippery leaves coercing me to follow him—
reluctant as I was. The path must have been less than a foot wide,
and if he lost his balance, he would have fallen down the cliff. He
was just wearing flip-flops! I don't think he cared for his life or
mine and would take me with him if he fell.

I was reluctant to follow him as I watched the sea smashing on
huge jagged rocks about thirty feet below and returned to the car
while he bellowed at me to come back.

Another life-threatening incident was on a horrendous holiday
down south. He insisted on driving but took delight in trying to
frighten me by deliberately slamming his foot on the brakes at
high speed causing my neck to jolt—or racing recklessly around
deceptive bends on a windy, coastal road. I realised then he was
unhinged—and to be honest with you, I have felt a kind of release
now that he has gone, but not happy he had to kill himself. My
marriage was a complete sham.'

Belle wanted to give Cherie a hug but pulled back. 'Poor girl—
we had no idea you have been through so much. If only we knew,
we could have been there for you when you were on the farm.'

'I'd been totally deceived by him from the outset and was also
self-deceived into believing he was someone he wasn't. I was too
embarrassed to let on to anyone and never revealed to my
parents any of the abuse during my entire marriage. Tom was so
clever at putting on an act around my parents, but Tom's mother,

who I think had guessed what was happening, supported me. I guess she always hoped he would come right.'

Milton wound up the counselling session.

'Sounds like you were released from what could have been a life of hell on earth. God is on your side, Cherie and don't you ever forget it.'

During Cherie's stay, her parents rang to say they'd found a buyer for Ambury Farm and her father handled the legal matters in negotiation with Tom's parents. The new owners took over a few months after Cherie left Peace Haven.

Chapter Twelve

When Belle opened the mail at Peace haven, amongst it was a Thank You card with a photo of Cherie baring a beaming smile holding Ruby.

Cherie looked just as she appeared to Belle on her exit from Peace Haven with glowing cheeks and shiny red hair—a picture of health.

She wrote ...

Dear Milton and Belle

You will never know just how much it meant to me, all that you did to enable my healing. You went out of your way to make my time with you comfortable and welcoming.

Belle's special touch in the ensuite and bedroom, delicious homecooked food each day and Milton's prolific words of wisdom and guidance during my counselling sessions enabled me to recover much faster. One day I'll tell Ruby how you helped her when her daddy died.

Once I settle into my new home, I'd like to come and stay with you again, if that's okay.

I'm with my parents in Winton Abbot and they're helping me buy another home so I can be close to them, my work and Ruby's pre-school.

My love to you all, God Bless

Cherie and Ruby

****

Belle and Milton needed a break before the next lot of guests arrived. They loaded their kayaks onto the roof-rack, packed a lunch and headed off towards the Lumley River near the local cheese factory.

Belle loved the location—especially the gelato ice-cream parlour in the tiny village of Lumley.

The river meandered towards a dam which used to be an active Hydro Power station, but no longer in use. Wildflowers grew along the riverbank, especially in spring.

The highlight for Belle was the Friesian cows staring at them from the side of the river bank with dreamy brown eyes and long eyelashes. The coloured kayaks passing by with humans fascinated them.

For Belle, an even greater bonus was the baby calves standing next to their mothers watching with bewilderment.

Belle fossicked inside her dry-bag, taking out her camera.

'Milton, Could you hold my kayak steady while I take a photo of that cow with her calf?'

'Why don't you paddle in front of them and I'll take the photo while they're looking at you after I steady your kayak.' Milton paddled behind Belle and then took hold of the nose of the tail of her kayak.

The weather was perfect—absolutely wind still, just how Belle liked it. The sun gently warmed her soul and as she gazed at the bright, blue sky and her surroundings, she imagined they were in paradise.

They pulled into a narrow inlet with a flat grassy area where they could disembark.

'I'll grab the basket with the food Belle. We could sit over there under the willow tree. The sun is too hot.'

Milton walked over and sat under the tree, unpacking the food from the basket. 'Mmm, I see you packed my walnut brownies, thanks, Belle.'

'I was going to pack some of that roast chicken we had last night, but I'm glad I didn't now that it's so warm—it'll perish in this heat. Instead, we've got cold lamb sandwiches with that wholegrain bread I baked last night, full of seeds—sunflower, sesame and flax.'

'Thanks for that synopsis, Belle,' Milton said with a chuckle. 'I know you hold your organic natural cooking in high esteem, and so you should. It's kept us both healthy so far.' He gave her an endearing wink.

'Well, I was raised to believe you are what you eat!' Belle said with conviction.

'So, if I tuck into these walnut brownies right now, will I become a picture of health?' he goaded while taking a second brownie.

'I made cold lemonade too, flavoured with fresh mint which I've kept cold with ice packs.'

They set off after resting under the willow for a lunch. The trip to the dam and back to the carpark took about three hours, not including the lunch stop.

Belle felt relieved to arrive back at the boat ramp. 'I'm afraid I am not as fit as I was the last time we did this.'

Milton prodded her waist. 'That was two years ago wasn't it? Too much time spent indoors with the guests, Belle. I'll have to get you mowing all the lawns.'

She swatted him playfully with the end of her paddle.

'Oh yeah, very likely Milton—except I would rather chase you around the paddocks.'

They fastened the kayaks firmly onto the roof-rack and headed off to Lumley village which was a tiny tourist spot alongside the river.

At the village, there was a line of shops—a cheesery, craft shop, historical pub and ice-cream parlour, situated amongst popular strawberry market gardens.

Milton followed Belle as they took their strawberry waffle cones down by the river and sat on the steps, watching a mother duck with her newborn ducklings swimming by.

'What a perfect ending to a special day,' Belle said looping her arm through Milton's.

****

Later that evening, they sat enjoying the stillness of the night, reminiscing until the random mooing of Murray's cows broke the silence.

'I've been thinking we should get out more often and could stay at Shoal Cove for a few days. We haven't been there for months and I need to do some outside painting. If we don't look after it, the wood will rot.'

Belle gave a half-smile. 'Sounds like a good idea but it's only more work for us if we just go there to do maintenance—no different than if we stayed here.'

'Well, it's still a change of scenery. It's just that it has been in the family for years. My grandparents owned it and maintained it well and now it belongs to me, so I feel a responsibility to look after it for future generations.'

'I guess you're right. I'll check the bookings and see when we have a gap,' said Belle, wondering if they would ever get a break. She went to the office to get the register.

'We have that chap, Selby coming to stay. The one I told you about who had a horrific motorcycle accident years ago. There was an article about him in the Taupo Farmer's Monthly Magazine which his mother sent me. I forgot to tell you—here it is.'

'Oh, that's right, what actually happened? I can't remember the details.'

'Have a read, Milton— it's really incredible he's still alive.' Belle handed him the newspaper.

Amazing Rescue Story

Taupo Farmer's Magazine – July Issue

Selby lived on a sheep farm just outside Lake Taupo with his parents. He had just graduated from Senior College at the age of eighteen and looked forward to the summer holidays. He loved to ride his motocross bike on the dirt track that ran parallel to state Highway Seven.

One fateful morning, he donned his helmet and set off for a good blow out which he hadn't done since before his exams had started. Now they were over, he was chafing for a taste of freedom.

'See ya Mum—I'm off for the morning.'

'Okay, Selby—but remember you promised your father you would help drench the sheep at three today,' said Hilda his mother.

Selby became irritated at her reminder. 'Yes, I know—I remember.'

'I packed you a big lunch.'

'Cool thanks, Mum. I was going to buy a meat pie and a coke.'

'None of that now, Selby. That muck won't do your health much good! Especially if you're wanting the Police to be accepted for the Police Academy.'

'Right, Mum. Tell Dad I'll be back by three.'

Three o'clock came and no sign of Selby.

'Arthur!' His wife, Hilda stood in the doorway appearing agitated. 'Selby promised he would be back to help you by three. You know we can always take him at his word.'

Arthur tried to reassure her. 'Don't worry Hilda, I'll bet he didn't check his fuel tank before he left. He's conked out before— remember the time his fuel ran out in the state forest?'

'I know that could be the case. Even if he had his radiophone with him, I doubt whether he could get any connection in the forest. Even so, we won't find out for hours, will we? Just like the last time when he had to push the motorcycle home.'

Little did they know that later that day, their whole lives would completely change forever.

Selby had been having the time of his life. The freedom he felt with the wind in his face, tearing up and down the hills on the dirt track was so exhilarating that he couldn't hear the sound of another motorcycle coming from the opposite direction.

As the bikes both reached the top of the hill—bam—crash! The chilling sound of metal upon metal at sixty kilometres per hour and a sickening bang so hard that the cars on the nearby state highway could hear the impact.

The crash had been heard by Dan, one of the forestry workers a short distance away. He fearfully approached the carnage— bits of metal strewn everywhere—the blood from the bodies and the screams. One of the mangled victims lay silent, while the other screamed for help.

Dan made sure the quiet one was breathing and didn't require resuscitation then called for help on the emergency radio in his truck.

He could see that the young man who screamed had almost lost one arm which was hanging and pouring blood. Dan took off his T-shirt and tied it around the arm to control the bleeding.

Blood spurted from the other fellow's mangled leg that had a huge gash with bone poking through. He ran to his truck and grabbed another garment then wrapped it around the leg.

He checked his pulse. The forestry workers were all trained first-aiders, and he recognised the fellow was unconscious but breathing. He had not been wearing a helmet.

Dan then brought back water and pain-killers for the victim with the injured arm. 'What's your name?'

'Bobby Mitchell,' he moaned. 'How long will the ambulance be?' he whined, grimacing.

'It's not the ambulance—you'll be airlifted by Rescue Helicopter to the Army Base Hospital, as it is quicker—my name is Dan, by the way.'

'Oh—thanks, Dan, my arm is hurting like hell on earth. Thanks for the pain-killers though.' Bobby closed his eyes, his face contorted with agony.

The paramedics arrived, and the two men were airlifted to the hospital. Both men had lost volumes of blood and were given intravenous fluids during the trip. The outcome was horrendous.

The staff commended Dan on his heroics, and his boss had been informed of his valour

Selby underwent an above-knee amputation, as his shattered leg had become gangrenous. He was able to have an artificial limb fitted.

Bobby was not so fortunate. His arm was amputated and could not be fitted with a prosthesis.

Both men endured a long hard recovery.

For many years Selby received intensive therapy to manage his traumatic brain injury and he lived on government assistance for many years.

Bobby became an accomplished artist using one arm and made a good income for himself with his art exhibitions.

Selby eventually became fed up with not being able to live a normal life at such a young age. He wanted so much to be able to earn an income by working, to get married one day and support a family.

His father took him on a trip to watch the Para Olympics. He was so inspired that, when he returned, he was full of enthusiasm and felt he did, in fact, have a future and became an award-winning swimming Paralympian.

Article by Joe Bennett

Chapter Thirteen

Selby's parents had separated after the accident, due to the stress on their relationship. It just couldn't withstand the multiple hospital visits so far from home. They sold the farm and moved near the City Hospital where Selby had been transferred after being initially treated at the Army Base Hospital. The change was too much for them.

As a result of this family crisis, Selby developed nagging guilt deep inside, that wouldn't leave him. He had been living in a duplex townhouse next to his mother in Winton Abbot. After his grandmother had bought him this home after his accident, he carried out odd jobs around the town—washing windows and cars for local people and becoming bored.

****

Selby heard that a friend of his had received help from Belle and Milton after a serious accident.

'Why don't you go and stay for a while at that lovely Peace Haven lodge that Joey told you about. They have experience with people who have suffered major trauma, and Milton is a highly renowned grief counsellor.'

'It's not counselling I need!' Selby snarled angrily. 'What I need is some decent work opportunities, someone to point me in the right direction at least.'

Poor Hilda had often been browbeaten by Selby and she needed a well-earned break.

'Well, I'm just trying to help, Selby. I've heard such good reports about what happens at that place—people returning home healed and restored after a time there.'

'I know, I know—I just need to think about it.'

'It's not some kind of cult or religious order. They take people from all walks of life. You know that Japanese couple who own the corner shop—they stayed there too.'

Selby suddenly took an interest. 'Oh yeah, that cool couple who always give me change for the bus when other shops won't. What happened to them that they needed to go there?'

'They were victims of that terrible earthquake and tsunami that killed thousands in Japan. They lost both their children who were amongst dozens of others who died at the school.'

'Man, that's pretty horrendous! Why did they come over here?' Selby asked.

'They already had family here and wanted to start over again. Their whole city was wiped out.'

'Wow, that's heavy. I suppose when you stop to think about it, there are always others worse off than yourselves.' Selby lowered his eyes, pondering what he just said, before going off to his room.

Selby's stubbornness annoyed Selby's mother but knew she had to let go and let him make the decision to go to the retreat himself—otherwise he would resent her.

****

After Belle and Milton arrive home from their short stay at Shoal Cove, Selby arrived.

'Well, I'm here in one piece after a bone-shaking trip in that small plane,' snarled Selby as Milton lifted his overloaded suitcase into his vehicle.

'Do you mind stopping at a Take Away somewhere—I'm starving?'

Milton sensed an attitude of entitlement in Selby's voice. 'I'd rather not, Selby. Belle has a decent lamb roast in the oven with roast potatoes and all the trimmings and she's doing it especially for you!'

'Okay—if you say so,' he mumbled in response.

When Selby arrived at Peace Haven, Milton showed him around and Belle allocated him a disability-friendly room near the dining room.

Milton had already planned an itinerary for Selby, which included a fishing trip on his friend's launch, and a visit to a neighbour, Murray who had some ideas for work for Selby.

'Well, I haven't had a decent lamb roast in a long while thanks—it was great,' Selby said to Belle, cleaning every last morsel off his plate and rubbing his belly.

'Hope you don't mind if I have some time out?' He excused himself to Belle and Milton and the other guests.

The next morning, he was up early, ready for breakfast and noticed Belle setting the large dining table.

'Can I give you a hand there?'

Belle could see that there was an affable side to Selby, in spite of his rough edges. 'Sure, thanks, Selby.' She handed him the cutlery. 'Murray is going fishing with you and Milton later and looks forward to meeting you.'

Milton took Selby over to Murray's farm with their fishing gear. Murray waited on the doorstep and greeted Selby with a handshake. 'Good to meet you, Selby, I'd like to have a good chat with you while we're fishing as I think I may be able to help you.'

Milton's mate, Barney arrived with his boat and the men set off. Belle had packed a basket of food and the weather was just perfect for an afternoon on the sea at Tanners Point, a popular fishing spot.

Selby hadn't had this much fun since before his accident. He caught a few whoppers with the help of the other men, and they worked up a healthy appetite.

'Let's pull into that cove over there,' said Barney, while pulling up the anchor. They rested in the calm waters and dropped anchor again.

Barney had already stripped down to his swimming shorts and jumped into the water.

'Ahh, lovely! Come on you blokes, in you get!'

Selby turned to Milton. 'Well, I'm going in—how about you?'

Milton was concerned and protective of him. 'Do you think you should … I mean … can you swim with your artificial leg?'

'Of course, I can swim, but not with the limb, of course—I have to take it off.'

'But will it be a safe thing for you to do? It's pretty deep, about six metres I'd say.'

'Milton—I train at the Olympic Pool in Winton Abbot three days a week and compete with the swimming club regularly. The rest of my body is intact and I'm fit—maybe fitter than any of you.'

Milton scanned his toned body with strong chest muscles. 'Hang on Selby, wait for me! You might have to rescue me—swim champion!'

The men had a great time together. They headed back to Murray's farm where they cleaned the fish and shared a few cold beers. Barney piled the rest of his things into his boat and drove off home.

'Milton—why don't you leave Selby here with me for a while and I'll drop him back in time for dinner. What do you think, Selby?' Murray handed him a glass of beer.

'Sure thing, mate—but if you don't mind, too much beer gives me a headache. Do you have anything else that's cold?'

'I have some of Belle's ginger beer she brought over last week.'

Milton climbed the gate and walked home with a bag of fish over his shoulder, waiting to see the look on Belle's face when he appeared with a huge amount of fish for the freezer.

****

Back at Ferndale Farm, Murray was busy with Selby, giving him some good direction.

'My mate, Ernie is the local chippie who does most of the carpentry around Cromwell Mead. He is looking for a hammer hand and someone with a lot of muscle like you.'

Selby suddenly found his voice. 'What kind of jobs?'

'Not big jobs—building houses or such like—just carpentry for the locals. He is willing to give you an apprenticeship once he meets you and knows he can rely on you.'

'Are you sure he'd be interested in someone like me?'

'I've told him all about you. I'll take you to see him tomorrow if you're keen. What do you think Selby?'

'Wow, man. I would never have thought of an apprenticeship. Though he might change his mind if he knows I have an artificial limb.' Selby pouted.

'No talk of that now—it's all sorted—he's keen to meet you and you can work with him a day or two to see how you like it and if you both hit it off.'

'I don't know what to say—it's an amazing opportunity I suppose, but I don't know—I'll have to find a place to stay out here and don't know if I can afford it.'

'Milton says you have a townhouse in Winton Abbot. You could rent that out and come and share my place with me. I've got plenty of room, and you could help around the property too. I wouldn't charge much, and you could also derive an income from your own place.'

'I couldn't do that—I don't want to put you to a lot of trouble.'

Murray looked at him with a wry smile. 'It wouldn't be any trouble. I was looking for someone to cook me a feed each night and polish my antique furniture.'

Selby's mouth dropped open, as he appeared to have taken Murray seriously.

'Naah mate, just having you on. Of course, I didn't mean it! I've been thinking of getting someone in to keep me company, I suppose. It's up to you. Try it out for a while, and if you don't like the setup, you can just leave—no ties.'

'Can I think about it and let you know? I'll give my mother a call tonight and see how she feels about me letting my house out, seeing she lives next door.'

Selby enjoyed his time with Milton and Murray the rest of the week that he almost forgot about the offer until Milton asked him if he was going to take on the apprenticeship.

'Ah darn! I forgot all about ringing Mum to discuss renting out my place and the rest of the news. I'll try and get hold of her.'

****

In the cool of the evening, as Selby stood on the veranda sipping lemon verbena tea, his eyes scanned the property. The hills in the distance appeared to be fire, reflecting the intense red sun sinking behind them. The radiant blue sky and lime green conifers on the hills stood out. A large wood pigeon noisily hurled itself off the branch of the elm tree above the veranda onto the kowhai tree.

He glanced at the lake—his eyes catching the silver, glistening ripples made by the gentle breeze. So still—tranquil. No wonder they named it Peace Haven.

Murray's property had a similar view with a sizeable lake fed by the same spring shared by Peace Haven.

A cloud of sadness descended on Selby at the thought of leaving his newfound friends and these beautiful surroundings. He sat thinking of what it could be like living with Murray and earning a decent income as a carpenter.

The thought of having to rely so much on his mother and getting bored hanging around Winton Abbot with not much to take his interest irked him. He came off the phone with a smile on his face as he wandered back inside for supper.

The other guests had left the lounge, and Belle and Milton sat together relaxing before clearing up.

Belle offered Selby a piece of his favourite carrot cake.

'Another cup of tea and cake?'

'No, thanks—the cake was great, though.'

'How did you get on with your mother?'

'Murray's offer blew her away. She thinks it's a perfect set up that could benefit both Murray and myself and she said she would be honoured to look after my place.'

'That's good news, Selby. You and your mother could get the prospective tenants checked out with a Police and Credit check.

She may even find someone through her church or by word of mouth—I wouldn't worry about that too much.'

'I'll rock on over to Murray tomorrow and tell him the news that I've accepted both his offers.'

Milton was elated at the outcome. 'Murray's coming over here in the morning to give me a hand to repair a fence. If you want to tag along, Selby, you could gain a new skill.'

Belle was equally enthralled. 'And I'm putting on another roast in the afternoon. You can ask Murray for dinner if you like.

'Good idea,' said Milton. 'Then Selby can discuss the finer details with him over dinner.'

Chapter Fourteen

The following week, Selby went to Winton Abbot to get his place sorted out to rent as a furnished property.

The noticeable change in Selby impressed his mother as she could see he'd lost his depression for the first time since his accident— enthusiastic about life after years of feeling useless and hopeless.

Hilda busied herself cleaning the inside of the house while Selby washed the windows and mowed the lawns. They decided to let an agent find the right tenant, especially a quiet and stable person to live next door to Hilda.

The following week, a middle-aged couple in their late forties moved in. The cottage was perfect for this childless couple who'd purchased a small café in the Botanical Garden, a popular venue with a high reputation for their home cookery.

'I'm an investor now,' Selby said to his mother with a grin from ear to ear.

'I'm so happy for you Selby. If Murray doesn't charge too much board, you can put the money towards your apprenticeship.'

Selby stayed with his mother until the tenants moved in then set off back to Cromwell Mead to move in with Murray, who picked him up in his new Dodge.

****

Murray tried hard to get a laugh out of Selby, who took everything so seriously. 'Hi, how are you mate? Heard you have a couple of goodies in that house of yours. Big time investor now, are you?'

'Yep—I have an agent looking after the rental— and Mum, of course, to help now and then.'

'Put your stuff in the room at the end of the house there. It gets plenty of sun—you'll like it. I hope you don't mind if my Border Collie, Maggie comes inside. She likes to lie on the hearthrug in the winter in front of the fire, and in summer she still does it, even when the fire's not going. Keep her out of the bedroom though, thanks.'

'So what's the plan?' Selby asked with a hint of entitlement again.

'You said you're doing your practical training with my mate, Ernie. What about the course—have you applied already?'

'Yeah, I decided to do it by correspondence. I can't concentrate long periods at a time, so that way I can get a break if I need one.'

'Well, Ernie is ready to start you off next week. You need to phone him to confirm it.'

'I already did that in Winton Abbot. He said he wants me to help him with the handmade furniture he sells at the big market in Winton Abbot and he's going to train me to do wood-turning. Says he'll pick me up on Monday morning.'

****

Milton and Belle sat in their swinging two-seater on their veranda, enjoying a cool breeze after a hot day. They were tired after a busy time entertaining a group of guests, who had just left that afternoon.

Milton sat pensively next to Belle who nestled into him. He squeezed her hand. 'Don't forget that the woman from Kenwick is arriving in the morning. Amelia is her name.'

'I know—I've been getting her room ready. She needs a lot of support.'

The next morning, Amelia's son, Tony dropped her off at Peace Haven. He had some work in Winton Abbot and stayed there in a motel overnight. This woman, whom Belle had met her several years earlier at a nurse's conference, was always immaculately groomed, in Belle's eyes. Although she had turned sixty, men still found her attractive for her years.

This time, Belle was astonished to find her friend bedraggled with tramlines in her neck, her face pale and drawn, and since Belle last saw her, grey dominated her thick mop of hair.

Amelia had booked in for extensive counselling sessions with Milton this time. Belle greeted her with a warm hug. 'Hi, Amelia, lovely to see you again—I'm so glad you held onto our brochure I gave you at the conference. We've had several nurses through here—mostly worn out.' Belle took her arm as they wandered inside the lodge and Milton followed with her suitcase and took it upstairs to her room.

'I'm so relieved to arrive and grateful that I had Tony to bring me down. He lives close enough to help me out now and then, but it still takes me an hour and a half on the bus to visit him.'

'Well I'm sure, after a decent rest and our support, you may be able to put things into perspective better and sort out a few issues,' Belle replied.

'Milton has contacts in the province who could offer you practical support. You would do well to make your needs known to him during your counselling sessions.'

'The first thing I'm going to do is take a nap after lunch.'

'Not until you try some of my chicken and cranberry quiche, I baked with fresh organic eggs I collected this morning.'

'Sounds wonderful. I heard you do a famous Devonshire Tea with your homegrown raspberry jelly.'

'That's for afternoon tea. I also make clotted cream for the scones.'

'Do you milk a cow as well?' Amelia asked with a chuckle.

Belle laughed. 'No, we get it from Monty, the farmer next door who swaps it for free-range eggs, or vegetables and fruit from our orchard when in season.'

'Wow, you have quite a little Co-operative going on here—sounds great!'

'Yes, I suppose we do. We also get a side of lamb now and then from our other neighbour, Murray. He gives us meat for eggs and berries or other fruit. We pay him to mow our lawns.'

Amelia settled into her room and slept soundly until mid-afternoon when she awoke to the sound of birds in the trees below.

As she wandered downstairs into the lounge, Belle arrived pushing a regal-looking white wooden trolley with cabriole legs on coasters out to the veranda. A tea trolley full of all kinds of culinary delights for afternoon tea.

Amelia perked up. 'Belle, let me give you a hand.'

'No, sorry, that's not on our agenda. You are here to rest after you've spent most of your life running after others.'

'Aww, thanks, Belle, that's sweet of you. If you don't mind then, I'd like to take a walk around your lovely grounds.'

'That's okay. I'll give our other guests their tea and we'll have ours with you in about twenty minutes, so take your time. Check out my gorgeous English country garden by the lake.'

Chapter fifteen

Amelia started her Restoring Past Foundations programme with Milton the next morning. He took notes as Amelia told her life story. He wrote ....

Amelia had endured a tough life. She had raised two sons and was so proud of them. They were the focus of her life until her marriage broke up when her sons were at Thames College during their adolescent years.

Arnold, their father, was a drop-down drunk, especially when he disappeared for days on end during a binge. He had been kicked out of the Air force as an engineer early in their marriage for drinking. Since then, he only worked sporadically between benders, but his hangovers were so bad, he slowly became incapacitated.

There was an eight-year age gap between her sons. Her husband had accused Amelia of getting pregnant to another man, saying that Tony was not his son. This was so untrue. Amelia was the most loyal, devoted and faithful wife.

He would not believe Amelia until she forced him to have a DNA test which came back conclusive that Tony was indeed his son, although he looked quite different from Larry, their firstborn.

Arnold had to believe her now, but he nevertheless continued to treat Tony with disdain as he was close to his mother and protective of her.

Larry had always been the apple of his eye and was spoilt rotten by Arnold.

Amelia worked hard as a part-time nurse, to pay the mortgage and take care of the boys while their father played the field— drinking and chatting up women in the pub.

When Arnold died of alcoholism before he turned fifty, Amelia had already left him after his drinking had become progressively became worse.

Larry took it hard and had resented Amelia for leaving his father, but his mother was at her wit's end. When he turned 17, he left home and become a regular hard drug user. By the time he reached twenty, he had developed irreversible drug-induced psychosis.

Amelia only survived these tumultuous years through the prayer and support of her local church while Larry remained in psychiatric care from his mid-thirties.

Tony had a Doctorate in Sociology and worked in research at various universities and tertiary institutions around the country.

He was concerned about Amelia and bought an investment property for her to live in, a small cottage in Kenwick Village, near Thames.

****

Milton wrote down all of Amelia's story during their counselling sessions and he and Belle also prayed with her.

'I am so pleased you decided to embark on Restoring Past Foundations, Amelia and, believe me, a huge weight will lift off you by the time you have finished the programme. It's a kind of emptying out of all the negative things of the past that weigh you down. When we finish, you'll have a new wineskin to be filled with new wine—only metaphorically, of course.'

'Thanks, Milton, though it does stir up painful memories when we delve into the nitty-gritty of it all. At times I just want to run for the door, but realise I need to be set free from bondage to my past.'

'You're right, and I can guarantee you will experience a healing of memories by the time we finish.'

Belle stood at the door knocking. 'Sorry to interrupt—the hour's up. Just letting you know morning tea will be ready in five minutes.'

The aroma of fresh-baked scones wafted along the passageway finding its way to Amelia's nose as she entered the dining room. Scones with strawberry jam and dollops of clotted cream along with butterfly cakes covered in swirls of pink buttercream decorated the top tier of the cake stand. Mini ham and asparagus quiches lined a platter below.

Amelia leaned over the delightful spread. 'I love the way your table cloth matches your bone china tea-set. You've been busy setting this up.'

Belle placed her hand on Amelia's shoulder.

'I thought I'd do something special for you and I like to do this when guests come who are in need of a special touch. The rest of our guests have gone out so we have the afternoon to ourselves.'

'Goodness, where did you learn to make those gorgeous cupcakes?' Amelia asked.

'I attended a few classes of cake decorating at night school when I used to run a catering business from home.' Belle replied.

As they sat down at the table, Belle nodded her head towards the cottage where Annie lived.

'Amelia, I'd like you to meet Annie who lives over there in the cottage. Like you, she has also been to hell and back. She's going to pop in for a cuppa now too.'

Belle looked over at the cottage where she could see Annie shooing the hens off her herb garden. 'Looks like someone forgot to close the side gate.'

Belle called to her from the veranda, 'Annie, come and meet Amelia.'

After a hearty tea, the women went for a stroll around the lake. Annie stopped and took Amelia's hand. 'Murray and I are going to Penguin Bay for a picnic later. Why don't you come with us? I'll pack food for all of us, and I know Murray won't mind.'

'Oh, that's kind of you,' Amelia answered.

Belle shot a disapproving glance at Annie. 'I don't think Amelia could cope with that trip driving on a windy road in Murray's Dodge.'

Annie laughed. 'I couldn't cope with driving these windy roads in Murray's Dodge myself! I wouldn't put Amelia through that. No—Milton mentioned to Murray that he could take the van, so why don't you both join us?' Annie asked Belle.

'I'm sorry, not this time. We have a busy time coming up with the orchard—a heap of fruit needs picking and bottling,' Belle replied.

'I'll help—you know I will,' Annie insisted.

'No thanks, Annie. I'd like you to take a break—you haven't been off the property for a while.'

As usual, Belle acted like a super-woman, but she knew her own limits and asked for help if she needed it. In the the past, everyone knew her to be a people pleaser and had few or no boundaries. She had learnt her lesson when she became burnt out trying to cope with shift work as a nurse, managing ailing parents and tumultuous disastrous relationships with needy men.

But that was her past and things were different now that she had a strong faith, listening to that still, quiet voice within.

****

Murray drove the mini-bus cautiously around the deceptive bends along the coast road until they arrived at Penguin Bay. It was a glorious sunny day, not a cloud in the sky and absolutely wind still.

Murray scrambled out of the van unloading the folding chairs while the women took out the picnic baskets, unpacking the food that Belle and Annie had provided.

Murray jerked his thumb towards a patch of grass. 'There's a shady spot under those Pohutukawa trees over there.'

The three of them were relaxed and at ease with each other and by the end of the day, it was as though they'd known each other for years as they shared their life stories together.

'Wow, have also had a pretty rough time of it, Amelia—I'm so sorry to hear that. What a blessing you have such strong faith as we have. Murry and I have both recently done the Alpha Course, which changed our lives and made us much stronger to deal with life's powerful blows.'

'I've done that too! It helped me so much as I was struggling with my faith until then. I'd had enough of being knocked down in life, time after time and the way Nicky Gumbel explained things helped me come into a personal relationship with God. My son, Tony and I visited relatives in London for a few months and attended Nicky Gumbel's church in Brompton. It was an amazing experience.'

They sat around soaking in the afternoon sun and spectacular weather, sharing testimonies of their spiritual walk.

Murray started to fold up his chair, trying to give the ladies a hint to head home.

'Well, I'm done in. I have to get up early tomorrow and shift some sheep before the vet comes to vaccinate them.'

On the way back to Peace Haven, Annie sat in the bus chatting with Amelia who handed Annie a packet of chocolate jelly fruits. 'It sounds lovely the set up you have living at Peace Haven, Annie. The tight community you have all created is enviable—just like one big happy family.'

Annie sensed the loneliness in Amelia's voice, perhaps even a feeling of isolation. 'How often do you see your son, Tony, Amelia?'

'Not that often—only once every few months when he has a research project in Auckland and he'll stop by on the way through. I can't handle the traffic driving to Hamilton, now. The city has become so congested like and I'm glad to keep away from it.'

'What about Larry—do you see him much?'

Amelia's eyes welled up with tears, trying to contain herself while staring out the window at the sea. 'Yes, when his Mental Health Worker brings him to see me from Thames once a month, but his conversation is very limited. He now has a damaged liver from Hepatitis C which he contracted from using dirty needles when he abused drugs.'

Annie sensed the tragedy of Amelia's life—so much pain— and felt a strong urge to offer assistance, but how?

'I expect you are lonely living in Kenwick without any family around you.'

'Yes, I do—but I just have to make the best of a bad situation. I always tell myself there are a lot of people far worse off than me. My sister Fran lives down south and visits occasionally, but her husband has a business that ties up most of the time.'

'Do you have to stay in Kenwick? Perhaps you could move where you have friends or more of a community,' Annie suggested.

'I suppose I could, but I can't really afford to buy a house anywhere else and Tony owns my home. It is his investment property, and I just pay minimal rent.'

The three kept silent for the rest of the trip back home while Annie choked back the overwhelming empathy she had for her new friend who sat with her eyes glued to the window for the rest of the trip. Annie kept hands-off, at least at this stage of Amelia's recovery when she would be best left in Milton and Belle's care.

Chapter Sixteen

Annie sat at her dining table in deep thought waiting for Murray to arrive to pick her up. She recalled a conversation she had with Belle and Milton earlier in the week. They spoke of subdividing the land where Annie's cottage was located, and then offer it to Annie to purchase as a small block with the cottage and three acres.

Although Annie had received the pay-out from the earthquake insurance, if she purchased the property it wouldn't leave much for her future, although the offer from Belle and Milton was reasonable. Murray told her he wanted to discuss an idea he had an invited her out for a meal that evening.

He arrived in his Dodge, having given it a good clean out, especially the front seat. He'd placed a fragrant atomiser inside the vehicle to hide all kinds of animal odours.

Murray beamed as she stood in the doorway of the cottage tastefully dressed in her Ming blue cotton skirt and top, stylish white open shoes and a white merino shawl draped across her shoulders. 'Is that really you, Annie?'

She had paid extra attention to adorning herself with subtle makeup, appearing much younger than her years. She blushed and tried to change the subject quickly.

'What was that restaurant you said you are taking me too?'

'The little Italian job next to the Post Office. It does an awesome Chicken Linguine and amazing wood-fired pizzas. There is none to compare, in this area, at least.'

Annie enjoyed the close intimacy huddling up next to Murray in the front seat of the Dodge. He was a good driver and she felt safe next to him as he drove extra carefully with Annie on board.

The ambience of the Italian restaurant appealed to Annie and she wondered if Murray had specially chosen it for the romantic tables draped with starchy white cloths, the red candles, and mini vases containing mini rosebuds.

'Oh no—that's not Andrea Bocelli singing, is it? I haven't heard him for years,' Annie said, with a quaver in her voice. He was singing Time to Say Goodbye.

Murray ordered refreshments and while they waited for their meals to be served, he started the conversation.

'Do you still plan to move closer to your family in Winton Abbot once your insurance comes through, or will you will stay in the area?'

'We haven't really talked about it yet. I have kind of settled into life at Peace Haven, and they haven't mentioned it lately, as they know I'm happy here. They don't want me to feel obligated to live with them.'

'Annie ... Milton talked to me the other day ... about plans to subdivide the land where the cottage is and make it a separate title from Peace Haven. Did you know that?'

'Oh yes, they discussed it with me and asked if I'd like to buy it ... though ... they had told me when I first moved into the cottage that I could stay there as long as I wanted—but that was two years ago now. I suppose they thought I was going to move onto my son's property long before now.'

Murray hesitated then passed her the menu. 'Do you want any dessert? They have a decadent Tiramisu you might like to try?'

'Ah no—I don't think I can fit anything else in, thanks. The meal was delicious and quite filling.'

He stood up and lifted her merino shawl off the back of her chair, placing it across her shoulders.

'In that case—how do you feel about a stroll to the bay at the end of the road and watch the moon rising?'

'Sounds lovely—it's a good night for a walk.'

'I settled the bill when I went to the bathroom—let's go.' He took Annie's hand and led her down the street. She felt a strong sense of security and trust when Murray was close to her and this evening seemed to be special, as though their relationship had moved to the next level.

The palm trees on either side of the boardwalk, and the decorative terra cotta, plaster houses, gave a tropical feel to the evening. Annie imagined wandering through the streets of Italy or Spain with the love of her life. Is he the one?

At the end of the road at the edge of the bay, they sat together on a park bench watching the moon rise like a silver face smiling at them, granting its approval.

Murray turned to Annie, cupping her face in his hands and planted his lips softly on hers. She melted, mesmerised and motionless as if she hoped it would never end.

Annie wanted more of it but knew they needed to take things slowly. He wrapped his strong arms around her, shielding her from the cool sea breeze that began to form ripples in the moon's rays on the water as she leaned back yielding to his protection and overt displays of affection.

'Annie, I've been trying to get the courage to ask you something—something that could change our lives forever,' he said, with a slight stammer.

Annie looked at him with bewilderment. What was he about to ask—not the big question, surely? She was unprepared.

'What do you think about the two of us getting together … I mean for good … you know … tying the knot so to speak?'

He lacked confidence, and this was a brave step for him to take. 'I know I said to you, when we first met, that I didn't think I would marry again—but things have changed significantly since I met you.'

Annie's eyes darted away from the beads of moisture on his brow as his neck flushed.

'I've become familiar with your company—your great companionship and friendship. I've also come to know you as someone I can trust—as you are probably the most sincere, honest and open person I've ever met.'

'Oh dear, that may be a bit over the top—but thank you, Murray—I feel the same way about you. Though it does scare me somewhat, living with someone for twenty-four seven after living alone and having to cope on my own.'

Annie was intense, trying to find the right words that were hidden in her heart. 'Marriage means two people having to adjust to another's habits, idiosyncrasies and baggage from the past. I don't know if I have the strength to go through it all again. I'm afraid.'

'But this time you'll have the love and support of someone who genuinely loves you and believes in you for who you are—not what they can get, and as you said—it will need to be a God job.' Murray spoke with conviction. 'You said once that your husband, Nigel took you for granted and you often felt invisible.'

Annie tried to explain away her anxiety at getting married again. 'I know, but marriage is such a permanent thing and it takes a long time to really get to know a person if you don't live together before getting married. And I don't believe in de facto situations where it easy for a person to just walk away. On the other hand ... with marriage ... one could be horribly trapped if it fails. It is hell on earth going through divorce proceedings and all the stress involved—I saw my sister go through it.'

Murray looked at his feet, clearing his throat.

'So ... I suppose the answer is no—I'm really sorry I've made you feel embarrassed—perhaps I've made an assumption,' he said as his voice faded.

Suddenly, Annie confessed. 'Oh no Murray, not at all!'

Annie felt a full confession was needed in case she had frightened him off. She took his hands in hers and looked at him directly. 'I'm afraid I've fallen for you in such a major way, it scares me. You captured my heart long before this. Why do you think I keep popping over with cakes and offering to cook for you? Not because I feel sorry for you being a poor widower living alone, but because I want to be with you.'

Murray's eyes widened and the corners of his mouth turned back up into a radiant smile.

Annie continued. 'When I don't see you, I'm always thinking of when I'll get to see you next—it's just that I'm afraid of being disappointed again, that's all.'

Murray was lost for words at Annie's confession.

'Well, not if God is in control and we're not running the show. Neither of us had any faith in the past but now things are different. We could ask Belle and Milton for some feedback and prayer about this if you like.'

Annie hesitated, thinking of a way to ease her tension.

'We could keep going as we are, but as an officially engaged couple, and then further down the track when we are both ready, we can talk about a wedding date. What do you think?'

Murray wasn't sure about this idea but tried to sound confident. 'We could make a tentative date for twelve months, and close to that time, if either of us is not ready, we can extend it.'

'Wow, you've really been giving this some thought, haven't you?' she responded.

Murray wanted to bring the conversation to an end.

'I don't think we should string each other along, so it's a good idea to have that tentative date. We aren't a couple of teenagers, I know—but I'm not going to let you get away that easily.'

He pulled her closer for a kiss, determined to win her heart completely—but for now, this would suffice.

****

Belle and Milton were overjoyed with the news as they all sat together in the lounge with Annie and Murray discussing the pitfalls and benefits of marriage as they had experienced it, and how they worked their way through.

'I expect that, in all earnest, even when you really believe you are in God's will, our own humanness and self-will can still take over. None of us is without character defects and irritating idiosyncrasies,' said Milton.

'Well, I think relationships are all a risk one takes to love and be loved.' Belle added. 'There are no guarantees that we will always get it right.'

'People often say marriage and relationships are a gamble, a risk of getting hurt—or as the world says—of failing,' said Milton.

Murray interjected. 'I agree with what Belle said about taking the risk to love and be loved, or staying alone your whole life with no one to share your thoughts or experiences each day.'

Milton was suddenly stuck for words. There was quietness in the room for a moment and then he spoke.

'I honestly believe you two should go for it. It does seem obvious you are equally yoked in many respects, and you truly love each other.'

****

Belle and Milton went south for three weeks and enjoyed another memorable time with Rose and Andy. The twins were no longer babies and started pre-school. Belle was in her element taking care of them while Rose had more time to ride her horse around the station helping Andy.

While Milton and Belle were at Perendale Station, Annie and Murray had been hosting the retreat. They had no guests booked in for counselling and Murray attended a one-day training workshop in Crisis Intervention for farmers, run by Federated Farmers.

Amelia had left and returned for a second stay at the retreat just in time to help Annie and Murray out and by this time, they had set a date for their wedding,

Chapter Seventeen

Annie was pleased to see her favourite couple return from visiting Rose.

'How did it all go Annie?' Belle asked as Amelia offered them both a cup of tea and fresh muffins.

Milton winked at Belle. 'It must have been okay, as we had no urgent calls.'

'Don't you worry, Milton. We were the perfect hosts and Murray is a whiz in the kitchen, by the way! Cookie was off sick for a few days and Amelia helped me muddle through and made the most perfect omelettes and French toast. They were keen on my Shepherd's Pie, I might add.'

Murray walked into the lounge, overhearing the conversation. 'My ears are burning! I hope I'm not being hoodwinked into full-time kitchen duties now,' he chuckled.

'Annie and Murray—please stay for dinner. We could have a catch up on the last three weeks, or any bookings to discuss if that's okay,' said Belle.

Murray picked up his leather stetson that had been a gift from Annie. 'I need to shoot home and move some stock for the night and check the electric fence that's giving me trouble. I'll be back for dinner though, thanks.'

Later that evening, when the other guests had left the lounge, Belle and Milton sat out on the veranda with cold refreshments and freshly made chicken liver pate that Annie had made.

Belle handed the plate around. 'Try some of this on toasted sourdough which I've cut into cubes.'

Milton savoured the morsel. 'I think Cookie could be out of a job soon at this rate, Annie with that pate—or you could be a promising second chef into the bargain.'

'We had a call from Amelia who is arriving tomorrow. She misses the communal spirit here and says that since she last stayed, she realises how isolated she has felt. She would like to come back and discuss her options with us regarding her life choices.'

Annie had more to say but waited until Murray returned to join them.

Once they were all seated together, Murray announced the good news. 'We've decided to tie the knot in two months when the weather is settled. We'd like to ask you if you wouldn't mind officiating, Milton, seeing you're an official celebrant.'

'Great news, both of you. It would be a privilege.'

'We would like to book the lodge if you're able to do that for us. We'll pay the going rate, of course,' said Annie.

'Fantastic—a wedding!' Belle was elated. 'We haven't hosted one here for years!'

Annie sat looking out towards the lake at the spot where her friends and family would assemble in the Olive grove for the ceremony. The dark red roses were in full bloom, climbing on the picket fences.

Belle leaned over and touched her arm. 'Are you still with us, Annie?'

She startled as she was drawn back to the real world.

Milton disappeared into the office with Belle and returned with the booking register with her in tow.

Murray appeared eager to get things sorted. 'How do you feel, Milton? Are you able to officiate?'

Belle glanced at the register with Milton.

'We are free for a fortnight during that time. It is usually quiet a month before Christmas before they start ringing to make bookings for January. We close over Christmas to make way for our own family,' said Belle.

'I would be honoured to officiate,' said Milton. 'However—Belle and I had a word together in the office just now and will not hear of you paying for this. It will be our wedding gift to you both.' Milton wrote their names in the register. 'We feel we owe you so much for all the help and support you have both given us since we started here. You are part of our community now, like family.'

Their generosity overwhelmed the betrothed couple more than they could put into words.

****

After Amelia arrived back at Peace Haven again, they all sat around in the lounge chatting while she settled into her room.

'There is something else we would like to discuss while we are all together.' Belle prodded Milton. 'Do you want to tell them?'

'Yes, of course. Annie—regarding the offer we made to you to buy our cottage now that it has got its own title—would you still be interested now that you are getting married?'

Annie turned to Murray. 'Shall I tell them what we have decided?'

Murray squeezed her arm. 'Sure—go ahead.'

'I'll be moving into the house at Ferndale with Murray after we're married and we've been discussing the possibility of us both buying Lavender Cottage. Amelia could rent it, just as I have been doing all this time.'

Belle stood looking out the window where she could see Amelia throwing grain to the hens.

'That's a great idea, don't you think Milton? Seeing that she spends such a lot of time working in the kitchen, we don't want to lose her and it appears she has really made herself at home here.'

Milton craned his neck to join Belle spying Amelia through the window.

'I think we could let her stay for low rent and continue to pay her a wage for her kitchen duties and looking after the hens if that suits her.'

Belle waved her hand. 'She's coming this way. Why don't we call her in for afternoon tea and tell her the good news?'

Amelia walked inside carrying a fragrant bouquet of colourful freesias for the dining room table. Annie passed her a boysenberry cupcake with her tea.

'Amelia, we have something to tell you which may put a smile on your face.'

Amelia put her cup back down, wide-eyed.

'We're going to live at Ferndale Farm when we get married in a few months and will soon purchase Lavender Cottage. We would like to offer it to you at a low rent if you could also take care of the hens and collect the eggs each day.'

Amelia's face lit up like a Christmas tree.

Milton interrupted. 'And of course, we would still need you in the kitchen if you're happy to continue on wages.'

'I would be delighted! That's an amazing offer, thank you! I love that posh room and ensuite you put me in, but it's a while since I've lived in my own little space though. The hens already know me well too and I know all their names.'

She tried holding back her tears of joy to no avail.

Milton looked at her warmly. 'There's plenty of life left in you yet, Amelia—a whole new life. We have enough going on here to keep you busy for a lifetime. When you've had enough of us, you can always take up that offer of going to live with Tony and his family.' Milton said.

'You're a champion baker, Amelia. I hope you won't leave me in the lurch in the kitchen yet. And what about my herb garden you have been so carefully tending? I've never had such healthy herbs— we couldn't do without you,' Belle added.

'What can I say to all that. Looks like I'm part of the furniture now.'

****

Amelia's whole countenance had changed. She walked back to her room, thinking about all that was said with tears in her eyes, overcome by gratitude and a sense of joy and hope that she had not felt for many years. Sitting on her bed, she closed her eyes and gave thanks to her creator, God.

Sitting in her armchair, she reflected on what Belle had said about her baking, and the time she'd owned a little country café with her ex-husband, Arnold near Thames. It was known for its award-winning home-made pies and remained a popular item in the area until Arnold's alcoholism put an end to that.

The phone ringing intruded on her reminiscence. She rushed to the phone to speak to her son, Tony, who sounded relieved that the pressure of responsibility for his mother had been lifted off him and his wife Leila.

'We had discussed building a self-contained flat on our property to support you, but we thought it might be difficult for you to make the change now—I'm sure you are happier where you are rather than start over again trying to make new friends in Hamilton.

Did Tony say this to appease his guilt? Nevertheless, for now, she was more at home in the community of Peace Haven where she felt loved and needed and she wasn't sure she could cope with hectic, city life.'

Amelia stayed at the lodge until the day of the wedding. There was so much to organise for Annie and Murray—streamers to be made, cupcakes to bake and put into the freezer and discussions to be held about dresses for the bridal party.

The day before the wedding, Amelia and Belle were frantically busy baking and freezing finger foods.

Belle picked up each cupcake to check them. 'Amelia—how many cupcakes have you made already?'

Amelia retied her apron. 'Last count sixty-eight. I still have another dozen to make, that's all.'

Belle picked up the icing bag. 'Let me help you ice them.'

Amelia arched her back, holding her sides. 'Not until I've gone for a walk—I need to stretch my legs. Let's have a cuppa and come back to it in an hour.'

Annie walked in to see how things were going.

Amelia pointed at Belle. 'Look at superwoman over there—she just can't stop,'

'Don't worry—Belle knows how to listen to her body.' Annie reassured Amelia.

'I'm going to try on my outfit later. Why don't you two come over to the cottage for a hen's party?' Annie said.

'Not too late though. We all have a big day ahead tomorrow.' Amelia replied in a motherly tone.

****

Annie woke the next morning to a perfect day. The men had decorated the lodge, while the women were in the cottage. There were garlands of sweet-smelling frangipani everywhere, Annie's favourite flowers. When she drew back the curtains, the sun poured through her dining-room window and the sky displayed a clear, intense blue. She felt blessed.

Belle and Amelia raced over to help her with last-minute grooming. Annie had been to the village hairstylist the previous evening, who had sprayed her hair so much one could crack a nut on it. She looked radiant in her midnight blue gown with silver jewellery and white accessories. The dress, a stylish tailored satin, showed off her trim waist. The women helped put the garland of tiny white chrysanthemums in her hair, as the hairstylist had instructed her.

Murray was nowhere to be seen, as Milton was busy helping him with his last-minute grooming, making sure he didn't get stage fright and run.

The bridal party waited for the couple by the lake, right where Annie had visualised they would be under the olive grove. There were white wooden benches scattered around for the guests who needed a seat. The climbing roses on the wooden gazebo were in full bloom, providing a colourful setting for photographs.

Milton was the right person to conduct the ceremony.

'It's as though our circle of love here at Peace Haven is complete,' Annie whispered to Murray during the service.

It was a simple and short service, just what Annie and Murray had wanted—a no-fuss ceremony.

Chapter Eighteen

Annie finished packing her suitcase for the flight. 'Milton was the perfect celebrant, wasn't he? There were no hitches and everything went according to plan. It was idyllic!'

Annie was excited about their new life together. They both tried to grasp the reality that they were indeed now husband and wife.

Milton drove the newlyweds to the airport for their tropical honeymoon in Tahiti. 'I'm so excited,' said Annie. 'I've never had a tropical holiday before.'

'Hey, you two lovebirds. Which entrance should I use?'

Annie pointed to a large building. 'International Departures over to the left. Just pull up at the drop-off point.'

****

Back at Peace Haven, Belle and Milton loaded the boxes into the Land Rover that Annie had packed. Milton had offered to take them to Murray's farmhouse so that Amelia could move into the cottage right away. They left the cottage furnished for her as long as she needed it and Tony arrived to help her with the shift.

 'Why don't you stay for lunch?' Belle asked Tony, wanting to get to know him more.

'I can't today, as I'm working on a contract in Winton Abbot this afternoon. Thanks, though!'

'I believe you are staying in Winton Abbot before returning to Hamilton. We'll be welcoming the newlyweds with a lamb on a spit, kindly donated by Murray's flock. Why not join us?'

'That sounds awesome—I'll look forward to that. I'll bring some wine.'

'Don't worry about that. Murray has some pretty famous peach wine he made from our own fruit last season. Amelia told us you like your wines, so you should enjoy that one.'

'I'll sure be there, thanks,' he said warmly.

****

A month later, Amelia had settled into Lavender Cottage and Murray and Annie were at home at Ferndale Farm.

Early one morning Annie wandered up the crushed shell path at Lavender Cottage to visit her friend.

 'Amelia!' 'Where are you?'

Amelia appeared from the side of the cottage beaming a broad smile, carrying a basket of freshly laid eggs. 'You are just in time for a Spanish omelette. Stay for lunch and a catch up about your trip.'

'That would be good—I was about to give you a few tips about the management of those hens, but you seem to have it all under control.'

'Oh, no I haven't—I could do with some tips.'

Annie sat at the dining table looking around the room, observing that Amelia hadn't wasted time putting her own impeccable, personal touch in the cottage. She admired the elegant tablecloth with fine crocheted silk edges that created an heir of eloquence to the room.

Amelia had swapped the curtains with drapes she had chosen with an artful eye to match her linen upholstered furniture. Overall, she had created a warm and homely ambience—a delightful welcome for any visitor.

'I thought I should warn you about some of the tricky hens you have there—especially the large Brown Shaver and that dopey Plymouth Rock,' said Annie. 'Both of them like to hide their eggs under the bushes, next to that row of conifers along the fence. I found some rotting there once.'

'Oh, no worries there—I already caught them at it when I was searching for the hens. I count them now and have names for the ones that give me trouble,' Amelia said chuckling to herself.

'What names?' Annie asked intrigued.

'That Plymouth Rock I call Flapper, as she looks like she is dressed in Art Deco costume. The Brown Shaver is Nutcase, as she runs around like a chook with its head cut off. Naming them helps me to remember their peculiar antics so I can keep track of them. That Barnvelder over there is Woody after Woody Woodpecker, as she likes to give me a good peck when I go near her.'

'It looks like you have everything under control already, Amelia. Have you seen those awful Magpies that swoop down to eat the hen's food? That's why I erected that scarecrow along the fence-line that seems to keep them away.'

'Yes, I laughed when I saw the broom and trousers stuffed with straw. I'm not sure who the face is supposed to represent though.' Both the women laughed as they stood looking at the scarecrow trying to guess who it resembled.

'How are things at Ferndale Farm, Annie? Have you two love birds settled in? I hope you're enjoying farm life.'

'It's wonderful—just what I had literally dreamed of and never thought could happen.'

'Oh, tell me more—it sounds interesting.'

'Murry is a gentle giant—so attentive and scared I'll break if I do any work.'

'That doesn't sound like you, Annie.'

'I managed to talk him round, and I'm riding the quad bike now and helping with the sheep. I sheared my first ewe last week and it went really well.'

'I thought that sort of work was for fit, young people. Be careful Annie that you don't wreck yourself.'

'I don't have to do it as Murray's farmhand does most of the work. I just wanted to give it a go, that's all. But I do help out with drenching and vaccinating.'

Annie's gaze shifted suddenly to the cattle on the ridge at Ferndale. 'I think Murray is going to make this year his last with carrying stock commercially, and will just keep enough animals for our own needs. He wants to slow down now.'

'Good idea! You need time for your relationship too, don't forget.'

'He made a good profit on the sale of the rest of the land to our neighbour, and we can virtually live off the interest. Then there is the money he gets for working for Milton at Peace Haven.'

'I heard they want you and Murray to take over the running of Peace Haven more and more. Is that right?'

'We said we would gradually get involved more and more as it becomes too much for them. I need to get back now, Amelia. Great to see you are happy here.'

Chapter Nineteen

After eighteen months, there were major changes in the air.

'Amelia, have you seen Belle?' Milton called from the veranda. 'She went into Cromwell Mead and the car is here but I haven't seen her since she returned.'

'No—sorry, she isn't with Annie either,' Amelia called.

Belle sat by the lake under a willow tree gazing into the glistening water, meditating. She sought divine inspiration and guidance.

'Well God, what should we do now? I know sixty is not old— but Milton and I have worked hard here at Peace Haven and I think we can do with a break from running the guest house.' She looked upwards, looking for a divine sign. 'But there is such a need here in Cromwell Mead and Winton Abbot for people who are worn down by life. It would be such a pity to abandon this service to the community. What are we to do? We could go and spend our retirement in our beach house at Shoal Cove, but I would hate to see this place fall apart and a greedy, capitalistic investor take it over to build something unsightly here. Please, God, help me with the right words to approach Milton. I know he wants to wind down now.'

Belle waited for that peace in her heart that would be a sign that it was the right time to approach Milton.

Milton met her walking back from the lake and wrapped his arms around her. 'What did you get up to today? You were away for ages and I began to get worried.'

He followed her into the lounge as she plopped herself onto a couch and stretched her legs out on an Ottoman footstool.

'Sorry love, I just had to get my feet up.'

Milton slumped back into the couch beside her.

'After I came back from the village, I sat by the lake for while praying. I needed some guidance.'

'Can you share it with me—perhaps I can help?'

'I was wondering about the possibility of handing the management of Peace Haven over to Murray and Annie, as they are such wonderful hosts and fit the role perfectly now that Murray has become a Crisis Counsellor.'

'It's really strange, Belle, as I've been thinking along the same lines myself and was worried you might be disappointed if I raised it.'

Belle breathed a quiet sigh of relief. 'You see—Murray told me last night that he was selling off most of the rest of his acreage to his neighbour who bought the rest of Ferndale.

'That's marvellous. How does Annie feel about that?'

'Apparently, she is stoked with the idea of spending more time at Peace Haven.'

'What's going to happen then?'

'If you and I are in agreement, they asked if we could have a meeting together to discuss a formal handing over of the management with you and me as their supporters or mentors.'

Belle appeared concerned. 'But what are you going to do then? I mean—are you giving up your work completely?'

'I'll still continue to do part-time counselling in one of the counselling rooms when I'm needed. I can even manage to do that from Shoal Cove, as it's not so far to drive.'

The two couples sat in the lounge after dinner the next evening to talk business.

'Murray and Annie—we've decided you're the only ones we want to take over Peace Haven. We know you've both had some painful life experiences, just as we have, and that you understand the clients who have suffered brokenness and shame—the shame that the world places on a person for so-called failure, in their judgemental eyes.'

Milton spoke with a deep conviction that they had made the right decision.

'We need staff who have real empathy, and who don't believe in political correctness, believing they have to blend into society in order to be accepted and to be held in high esteem. We need people who don't judge or condemn others for their mistakes or place them into a stereo-typed box so they become disempowered and invisible to society. We seek staff who have the courage of their own convictions, even if it means being a whistleblower—to make a stand and fight for the underdog. We believe we have found what we are looking for in you.'

Milton talked as though he was a presidential candidate, but Annie and Murray could see his convictions and intentions were obviously sincere.

Murray looked at Annie for reassurance.

'Wow! I don't know what to say. What about it Annie—are you unanimous in this too?'

'I suppose we fit the bill—and we're all such good friends.'

Murray leaned forward, resting his arms on his knees twirling his wedding ring. 'But we would hate to let you down, as you set this place up, both of you—right from scratch. It may be difficult to follow in your footsteps.'

'I think it's a wonderful proposition,' gushed Annie. 'I believe we've been led into a ministry to serve others, using our own gifts and strengths— just like Belle and Milton.'

'Well, there you have it—it appears our hearts are both unanimous on the subject. Where do we go from here?' Murray asked.

Milton picked up his record book and started entering data.

 'We'll need to do things formally. I'll give you both an offer in writing for the position with a Job Description and show you the financials etc.' He leaned over towards Murray to show him the software he used. 'I have accounting software and can manage the accounts and tax from our beach house at Shoal Cove, but you'll have to manage the budget. When you two need a break, you can close for a short period or we can relieve you. Amelia is great with the clients too, and of course, she has agreed to stay on in the kitchen, fortunately.'

****

Annie and Murray revelled in running the lodge and they were the perfect couple for the clients at Peace Haven. Belle and Milton remained Founding Directors.

The retreat became well known for the compassion, kindness and understanding offered its clients. People from all over the country made bookings. A holistic retreat to soothe life's woes.

Previous clients continued to request counselling sessions with Milton or asked if Belle was still there. Those who had been healed and restored back to normal told others about their experiences at this special sanctuary in the countryside of Cromwell Mead.

****

At the end of a long day, Annie sat with Murray on the veranda watching the sun go down, just as Milton and Belle used to do.

Annie rested her head on Murry's shoulder. 'It was great to have Belle and Milton over for the day. They seem to be really enjoying the respite—not having to get up early in the morning to guests or listen to all their problems.'

'I don't think they see it quite like that, Annie. Milton is a born counsellor and it's in his blood to help those who are suffering. In fact, both Belle and Milton have been born to help and rescue the walking wounded—I don't think they'll be able to keep away.'

'I see what you mean.'

'Annie—Milton raised something last night that he wanted me to discuss with you.'

Annie sat upright and eyeballed him. 'Oh, this sounds ominous.'

'You know how we discussed the possibility of selling our home and the rest of our land back to the farmer next door? Milton asked if we would be interested in buying Peace Haven, as long as we keep it as a retreat. It would remain a Trust and they would still help us out. Milton will continue with the counselling here—what do you think?'

'Oh my goodness—that's amazing! To think of owning Peace Haven!' Annie's eyes became whirlpools. 'It's a huge step, but we know what we are doing—nothing would change much. And it isn't a job, as you say—it's a special ministry—a kind of calling.'

'I'll need to give them an answer, as they want to give up the guest house now—after so many years of catering to people seven days a week, they need a break. Are you sure we can take it on, Annie?'

'I think it'll be good for us. We still have Cookie in the kitchen who does the early shift and Amelia is totally committed.'

'Belle and Milton are still available whenever we need them.'

'You are doing well too, Murray, with your Restoring Past Foundations programme and Healing sessions.'

'Thanks—I'll call Milton tomorrow and arrange a meeting to discuss the formal process and a price we can agree on.'

****

A month later, Annie and Murray returned from the lawyers with the Property Title in their hands. Annie was blown away.

'We are now the owners and Directors of notable Peace Haven retreat. I just can't believe it!'

Murray took Annie's hand. 'We must remember that it's nothing we have done—it's by the grace of God. Belle and Milton are the founders, and it is their inspiration and God's direction and guidance which started all this—we mustn't forget it. We're just servants continuing their work.'

That's what had always attracted Annie to Murray—his obvious humility and ongoing gratitude for whatever shape or form God's grace was delivered to him.

Annie pondered on all that Belle and Milton had done for them and the support they gave her after the earthquake wreaked havoc in her own life. She remembered Belle coming to her room when they felt the earthquake on the south coast. It had frightened the living daylights out of her. Belle was loving and caring—a huge catalyst in her healing.

****

Belle and Milton walked arm in arm strolling around the lake discussing the week's events. Belle stopped to look at the hyacinth bulbs she had planted along the water's edge. They were in full bloom, a radiant indigo colour and had multiplied. Nearby were African violets. She picked a few flowers for her dining table, inhaling the deep fragrance of the Hyacinths which she liked so much.

'We have fulfilled our vision, or my vision, Milton, and now the dream is being continued by Murray and Annie. But they will have different gifts and strengths to offer others and it will work for them too.'

Milton reassured himself they were doing the right thing.

'I agree—although it does seem strange having to pack up and move out. I know we're only a short distance away, but it seems such a wrench. I'm pleased we can come and go as we feel like they said.'

'We prayed for guidance and had a real peace about it, so don't worry, it will all go smoothly. We've already made our beach house, Seabird Lodge, into a homely sanctuary, Milton. The family is coming for Christmas, so we'll have lots of fun in the water with them with the extra kayaks we bought.'

Annie suddenly felt the breeze that rippled the lake as she wrapped her shawl firmly around her shoulders.

'Let's walk back now, it's getting cold.'

****

The move to Seabird Lodge went smoothly. The boys came down from Auckland with their partners for the weekend and did most of the heavy work and finished off with a swim in the bay. It was a king tide, and the sea was exceptionally warm.

Harry called out to Anna, 'Let's take the kayaks out before it gets dark. Where are Jimmy and Penny? Tell them we're going for a paddle and to come along.'

Later that evening, Milton got the barbeque going and Harry finished cleaning the fish down on the water's edge.

'We caught a few snappers,' he said.

'And we picked some good-sized mussels off the rocks earlier,' said Jimmy, carrying a bucket of them outside.

Belle placed a tray on the table. 'I made a fruit punch if anyone wants a glass. I put some of Murray's peach wine in the fridge if you'd like one—just help yourselves.'

Belle sat on the deck sipping a glass of ice-cold punch made from fruit from their orchard. 'I'm going to miss the orchard, but Annie says we can help ourselves to fruit any time we like and wants me to help her with the preserves now the fruit is ripe.'

'Mmm—I can see you spending a lot of time at Peace Haven still, Belle. They'll start calling me the Peace Haven widower.'

'Aww, come on, Milton, I know you miss the lodge too. Why don't we just see this as our holiday break from Peace Haven until we settle down?'

'What have you done with your ponies, Mum?' Harry asked.

'Annie and Amelia love them and don't want to part with them. Annie still gives the village children pony rides once a month, and I like to play with them when I am there.'

'That's great, Mum. I'm glad you haven't had to give up your animals entirely.'

'We discussed with Annie and Murray the possibility of regular house swaps when they have a lull at Peace Haven. That way we all get the best of both worlds.'

Jimmy gave his mother a hug. 'That's a great idea, Mum—good for you! I think you have a tremendous set up down here, and we just love coming too!'

****

Back at Peace Haven, Annie practised her culinary skills on Murray and Amelia when Cookie wasn't there as he only worked part-time.

Murray bellowed down the hallway, 'Annie, the phone's ringing and I'm fixing a tap in one of the ensuites.'

Annie rushed to answer it.

'Hullo, my name's Cherie. Can I speak to Belle, please?'

'Sorry, Belle and Milton have relocated to their beach house. We are the new owners.'

'Is that you, Annie—do you remember me? I was a widow with my baby and came to stay at Peace haven many years ago.'

'You mean baby Ruby whom I used to babysit? Your husband had that terrible accident and you moved to Winton Abbot. Goodness, that was about twelve years ago!'

Annie couldn't believe her ears. She had always wondered where Cherie had ended up.

'I've completed a degree in Social work and have a part-time job in Winton Abbot. I've been married for three years to Lyon, who completed a Social Work degree when I did. We studied together.'

'That's so exciting, Cherie—can I tell the others?'

'I'd like to come out to update them with all the news and hope to find work in Cromwell Mead, as I miss the country life. I have a Counselling Diploma and specialise in domestic violence. Someone told me there might be some work with the Cromwell Mead Women's Refuge and Women against Violence group.'

'Are you working at the moment?'

'I've been involved with the Women's Refuge at Winton Abbot and they say there is a demand for this work in Cromwell Mead. With all the stress the farmers have been under, there is apparently a high incidence of domestic violence.'

'Well, I can understand that. You only have to talk to Murray and Milton—they will tell you. Look—you'll need to talk to Milton and Belle, as they are still both Directors in our business. In fact—give me your phone number and I'll get them to call you. How old is your Ruby now—is she doing okay?'

'She's really well and turns fifteen next month. I told her all about you all—how you helped me get back on my feet. I'd like to help other women in the way that you all supported me.'

After the weekend, when the family had gone home, Annie and Murray paid Belle and Milton a visit to discuss Cherie's phone call. They sat around in the lounge discussing Cherie's plans.

Annie began, 'How do you feel if we employed Cherie as a counsellor for the women?'

'Sounds good—but what would she do with Ruby?' Belle asked.

'Cherie says Ruby can take the bus which stops outside her college. Cherie also sees a few clients in Winton Abbot twice a week so she could drop her off to college on her way through those days,' said Annie.

Milton, who had been quietly nodding off, sat up looking interested. 'I think it would be good to have an accredited counsellor as a backup for Murray. Peace Haven needs a female therapist, as we receive referrals from the Women's Refuges in the province. That would work perfectly.'

Annie's expression appeared quizzical. 'But what about Lyon, her husband? She can't be in residence at the lodge without her husband, can she?'

'Why not invite them both with Ruby for a meal this weekend at the retreat?' Murray nodded at Belle and Milton. 'Why don't you both stay for dinner too? We can all have a meeting with them to discuss it.'

****

Cherie and Lyon turned up on time on Saturday morning with Ruby.

Annie barely let the young girl get out of the car before she almost hugged her to death.

'Ahh, Ruby, come here and give me a hug! You're so beautiful and grown-up—I can't believe it's you.'

After they reminisced for a short time, they sat in the lounge while Amelia brought in a tea trolley.

There was the usual tiered cake-holder with the exquisitely iced cup-cakes and a plate of mini savouries. Amelia had done her best to make an impression.

Cherie told her story how she had a heart for abused and oppressed women and that God had given her a gift of reaching them and described their experiences in Bangkok.

'Lyon and I took part in great fundraising schemes to raise money for trafficked women in Bangkok. We took Ruby there when she was accepted in an exchange student programme for a year. We used all the money we received from fundraising and placed it in a Trust for our organisation called Rescue Net.'

Belle showed sudden interest as this type of aid work was close to her own heart. 'Did you have much assistance from others—I mean staff and support from home?'

'While we were there, we set up a programme to train women and girls who had been forced into prostitution to gain skills in work that would keep them out of the brothels.'

'Who did all the building work over there?' Milton asked.

'Lyon organised friends from the building trade here to go and train locals to build safe houses. The women also had training in sewing, weaving and woodwork from local people and the Net funded their education. I drummed up interest from humanitarian organisations and churches from several countries to become benefactors who made large lump sum payments. We used the money to accommodate women in safe houses run by the Net, which does not push religion but offers support and care for the women.'

'Who is running it while you're living here, now?' Murray asked.

'I go over there twice a year to monitor the projects. They have employed their own people to train the women in these jobs so that they'll get a wage at the end of their training. Part of the organisation works with the police to do a blitz on the brothels with men working undercover.'

'Tell us about your recent trip there, Cherie,' Annie asked.

'My Team went undercover to this terrible place in Pattaya that is filthy, full of rats and disease. Lyon went with a video camera and saw young children locked in an attic—the youngest a four-year-old girl.

The hostages in the brothel serviced at least thirty men a day and many were beaten and badly abused. One girl told me she had become pregnant and wanted to leave. The bosses threatened they would kill her baby if she left, and she didn't see her child for a year until she was rescued. They were forced to perform on dirty stained mattresses without covers or blankets—it was heartbreaking. The police arrested the brothel owners, and in the last blitz, they rescued scores of young children, including boys, and women.'

Belle's heart of mercy started to race. 'What happened after you rescued them?'

'We had to identify them, but many had been kidnapped off the streets of Nepal then trucked to the brothels in Bangkok and Kolkata and had no idea that they were in another country. Others had been abandoned by their families. It was so soul-destroying seeing young children with their minds, bodies and lives completely wrecked.'

Cherie struggled to recall the events. Large teardrops oozed their way from her eyes and down her cheeks as she wiped them with her sleeve.

Belle stared at her with concern. 'Oh, Cherie—how could you cope—all sounds so horrific? What a wonderful organisation Rescue Net is. Are you both intending to pay another visit soon?'

'No, not for a while—I have a heart for the abused here in New Zealand and work part-time for the Women's Refuge in Winton Abbot and Cromwell Mead. There is so much need in our own community that most people don't realise. I also need to help Ruby stay focused at school. She wants to do a degree in Social Work too and is a bright girl—a year ahead at school.'

Murray flicked through Lyon's Resume. 'I could certainly use you both here. If you would be interested in counselling the men, Lyon, I could train you to deal with the farmers myself.'

Murray perused his Resume once again.

'I see you've done quite a bit of crisis intervention over the years.'

'Yes—and I would be interested in doing it here with you. I only have part-time work in Winton Abbot and not in the area of work which feeds my passion.'

Lyon was unable to have children due to an injury he'd received in childhood. He was thrilled when he became Ruby's stepfather and did his best to be the father she'd never had. He loved and nurtured her as though she was his own child.

'Why don't you meet us all at Peace Haven next Monday? We can talk business and tell you how everyone fits in—how this

Peace Haven works. Each person who works here is special and has God-given qualities and gifts that serve our purpose well,' Milton said confidently, though humbly for a founding member.

****

When Cherie and Lyon eventually moved into the lodge, they were allotted two rooms with adjoining doors so that Ruby had her own room.

Cherie stood in the doorway to their bedroom as Annie approached.

'Hey, this brings back memories, Annie—this is where Ruby and I stayed about twelve years ago. How amazing is that? I remember waking from my afternoon naps when I was fatigued and low, watching you pushing Ruby around the lake in her pram to get her off to sleep.'

I remember that well—a special time.' Annie handed her a small vase of white chrysanthemums and coloured frangipani for her dresser and greeted Lyon as he joined the women outside the bedroom door.

'Lyon—if you get bored, our neighbour who bought our farm can always use a hand with the cattle at feeding time. Cherie told us you spent your youth on one of those big stations down South where Rose lives.'

'That sounds great—I'll go and introduce myself.'

'Wait for Murray—he knows him well and will introduce you to him.'

****

Amelia had more changes on the horizon when Tony and Leila moved to Gordonton, a rural village near Hamilton for Tony to take up his new professorial role at the Waikato University, but this time, Leila was expecting her first baby.

It was a permanent research role working from home. They purchased a lifestyle block with a large home in the country, and just as Tony had promised, this one had a cosy two-bedroom brick and tile cottage for Amelia.

Belle had arrived with Milton to see her off. 'Amelia—I can't believe you're leaving us.' There were lots of tears. It was a huge emotional upheaval for them all, but the team invited Amelia to come and stay anytime and help out in the kitchen if she felt like it.

She broke into a warm smile. 'I'm only an hour away, and I want you to know that something special has happened to me since I have lived here with all of you.'

'Oh no, what have we done?' asked Belle.

'You've helped me to find a peaceful haven inside of me—in my heart and soul. I've come to believe it's not something one can only find on the outside—it can only truly be found from deep within one's soul. You wonderful people—my second family—

have given me the tools to find this special gift. I was such a mess when I arrived here—so lost and now I am found.'

Belle and Annie tried hard to contain their sadness at Amelia's departure, so they wouldn't spoil her farewell.

Murray carried her bags out to the new car that Tony had recently purchased for her. 'It was kind of Tony to get this for you—Corollas are so reliable.'

Anne grabbed her, squeezing her half to death. 'Well, Amelia, you can still drive your little car out here to see us anytime.'

'Aww—This is not goodbye—you can't get rid of me that easy. I'll be in touch soon.'

****

With Amelia gone, Cherie and Lyon moved into Lavender Cottage which they rented off Annie and Murray who had already settled into the lodge.

Cherie stared out the window watching the hens fighting over their food.

'I don't know if I want to chase those crazy hens around the place, Lyon.'

'I don't mind—I'm a country boy—I'll do it. I'm sure they'll grow on you, Cherie. They each have their own personalities and Annie has written down all the instructions for us.'

'At least we haven't got the ponies to look after. It's good Annie wants to still take care of them. I'd like to get a cat now.'

182

'One thing at a time, Cherie—I thought you had a list of changes you want to make to the interior of the cottage—new curtains and painting the walls. Let's get through that first.'

'I know! It's just that I have waited so long to put my personal touch to something homely—if you know what I mean.'

'By the way—it's such a relief your parents have agreed to look after the tenancy of your house in Winton Abbot. If we save that rent, we could get enough together to take another trip to Thailand.'

'Hey—who's rushing ahead now?'

Belle and Milton were thrilled that Cherie and Lyon were the perfect couple to run the lodge and managing the counselling now that Annie and Murray had pulled back. They were relieved they could follow in their footsteps and keep the care going.

There couldn't have been a better couple to replace Belle and Milton, as Annie and Murray were slowing down. It was not easy rising at dawn to prepare breakfast for guests and be there in the evenings to entertain them and serve meals. Cherie and Lyon were young—full of energy and enthusiasm, and Belle saw them as a real blessing to Peace Haven and part of a divine plan.

****

Milton was busy doing repairs on the roof at Seabird Lodge. He and Belle enjoyed their new lifestyle at the beach and continued to assist Annie and Murray at Peace Haven. Now that they had a resident counsellor, there was not so much demand for Milton to be there as regularly.

Belle walked out with a pile of sandwiches and grapes.

'Milton, when are you coming down off the roof? Lunch is on the veranda table.'

They sat in the shade of the awning soaking up the panoramic view over Shoal Cove—a regular past-time for them— watching the beach-goers coming and going along the seashore below.

****

The following summer, Annie and Murray met with Belle and Milton to discuss something important. They walked into the lounge to see that Cherie and Lyon had been invited.

'I feel as though we've been summoned.' Milton said, laughing and sitting in his favourite rocking chair. 'Must be serious.'

'Yes, you're right—it's pretty important, that's for sure. I'm sure that what we have to say will be off considerable interest to you.' Murray winked at Cherie and Lyon.

Cherie started talking with high emotion in her voice, focusing her attention on Belle and Milton.

'It all started with the wonderful friendship you and I had, Belle—when my late husband, Tom and I were on the farm and I was pregnant with Ruby. The love and support you offered me thereafter completely changed my life after I arrived at Peace Haven. I was so broken and confused, but you helped me to

184

mend. Without judgement or prejudice—even when you probably suspected Tom had killed himself, you never once let on. The point is—it changed my life and healed me to such an extent that it gave me the same passion for helping the lonely, lost and broken-hearted—just like you and Milton.'

'Goodness! That's quite a legacy you attribute to us. Honestly, Cherie, it was not my doing, nor Milton's. We give glory to God. I believe he chooses people who've been broken by life to reach out to the walking wounded and enable them to heal in the same way they too were helped by others. Remember the story in the Bible about Joseph whose brothers beat him and thrown into a well to die. The Pharaoh's men found him and took him to the palace where he was made prime minister of the land. Because of his misfortune, he could help his own people during a famine. At the end of the story, Joseph said to his brothers who came begging for grain, As for you, you meant evil against me, but God meant it for good, to bring to pass, as it is today, to save many people alive.'

Milton cut in. 'Cherie, the hard times and brokenness Belle and I have endured prepared the way for us to have insight and understanding about the pain and needs of others. I think that's what Belle is trying to say, as I've also had the same experience.'

'Cherie—tell them the news. They'll understand on the basis of what you have told them—go on,' said Annie.

'Thanks, Annie.' Cherie directed her attention towards Belle and Milton. 'We've made an offer to Annie and Murray to purchase Peace Haven as they want to pull back, mainly from the guest house activities. We have made them an offer which they have accepted—but you are both directors, we need your signature and input,' Cherie said nervously.

'Oh my goodness, Cherie—that's marvellous news! I couldn't think of a better couple run the retreat.'

Milton fidgeted with his spectacles as they slid down his nose. 'How will you manage the counselling sessions with Federated Farmers? It could be difficult coping with that and your clients in Winton Abbot, Cherie.'

'I dropped those off a few months ago when I decided I want to focus my energies here at Peace Haven.'

Lyon interjected. 'I've already completed the counselling course that Murray did as Crisis Intervention Counsellor for the farmers, so that will be my forte. Cherie is setting herself up as a part-time counsellor for the Women's Refuge in Cromwell Mead. We have allocated a bedroom studio for these clients in crisis—if the need arises.'

Cherie appeared elated with the arrangements. 'We're going to be living in the manager's flat that Annie and Murray live in. It's like musical houses! They are moving into Lavender Cottage and will be available on-call.'

Milton's expression appeared sheepish. 'I have to confess that this plan was something we had suggested to Annie and Murray when they first told us they want to take a less active part in the running of Peace Haven.'

'I think we should be okay. Annie has offered to continue to do the baking, and we have our new cook, Manuel who is there on the dot of seven to do breakfasts—a gourmet cook at that!' said Cherie.

'And Murray wants to continue being ground-keeper free of charge,' Lyon said with a look of relief.

'I suppose you could still use an old part-time codger like me to help with the counselling if you are short,' Milton added.

'See—what did I tell you, Cherie? You won't be able to keep any of us away.'

'We are a community and that's that.' Cherie gave a joyous laugh.

****

Christmas arrived again. Harry and Anna brought their two, sweet daughters, Emily and Lola. They'd grown tall and were unusually well-behaved. Emily was outspoken and confident like her mother and Lola more reserved—a deep thinker.

Jimmy and Penny came with their two children, Bernie and Briar. Although boisterous, they were cute and kept everyone amused most of the time.

Anna and Harry both had their children around the same time as Jimmy and Penny, and the cousins virtually grew up together. Belle would often go up to Auckland and stay with both families to do child-minding.

Gabby and her husband, Russell made an informed decision not to have children. They felt there were too many children in the world, and it was not a healthy society. Belle realised there were people just not cut out for all the responsibility and self-sacrifice required when babies arrive. They must feel free to make that choice without stigma, she decided.

Tyler had arrived with his little family too. Elly could relax now, as Max and Milly were teenagers and could keep an eye on the little ones. They spent most of their time swimming and exploring the cove.

Rose and Andy made it this time, and the twins were as tall as their parents. Fleur displayed her father's temperament, and Pierre his mother's mischievous sense of humour. They loved hanging around their cousins, and all in all the children got on well together and looked after one another at the beach.

The Lodge was packed full. With stretcher beds and bunks everywhere it resembled a backpacker's lodge.

The holiday went quickly and Seabird Lodge was almost empty again. Harry packed the car full after enjoying Belle's ice-cold lemonade.

'Mum—don't you think it might be a good idea to extend this place—I mean, we could do with a few more rooms and extra space, don't you think? You said you want to keep it in the family, and it will get so much use from all of us.'

'I suppose your right—it has been a tight fit this summer.'

Christmas went by far too fast for Belle. She and Milton had enjoyed having their family stay at Seabird Lodge and after they had all left to go home the house was so quiet Belle could hear a pin drop. They were exhausted but it had been much fun.

They sat on the veranda making the most of the warm and balmy evening, discussing the past week's events.

'Milton, I feel as though God is telling us to extend our home, as our family have enlarged so much we can't all fit in comfortably.'

'I've been thinking about this too. Murray has a good friend who is a builder. I'll ask him to get his contact details for us.'

****

It took six months to finish the rebuild of Seabird Lodge. Belle sat on the veranda looking out at the sea, listening nostalgically to the seagulls flying overhead.

She turned to Milton with tears in her eyes. 'Milton ... I believe it has happened ... the vision I mean. God has really come through for us in such a way that I never thought possible. He made me promises years ago, and I know we are ageing, but he is never too late—his timing is perfect.'

She showed him the one verse in the Bible she had cherished through all her years of brokenness and strife. When she read the verse, it was as if God, himself was speaking to her—not in an audible voice, but in her heart. He was saying that she should write down her vision so that she would remember what he had said. Belle had kept that verse for two decades.

Milton handed her a small package.

'I forgot to tell you that there is mail for you.'

'I'm not expecting anything. I wonder who this is from.'

Chapter Twenty

As Belle started to open the package, her name jumped out in bold letters—

BELLE'S STORY
A Research Study into Traumatic Grief in Childhood
By Dr Miriam Appelby, PhD (Psychology)

'Well—this is a surprise.' Belle unwrapped the parcel revealing an impressive book cover with an image of a young woman looking across a meadow at a large, stone farmhouse in the distance.

'It's from Miriam, my old counsellor from Restoring Past Foundations. She used my story, with my consent, for her research project for her PhD—Doctor of Philosophy. She must have finally had it published. I guess she must be getting on in years now—if she's still alive.'

Milton appeared bewildered. 'Did she send it, or did someone else?'

Belle scratched her head, peering at the postmark.

'It's faded—I can't see where it's from. Miriam told me that if she was successful in getting the book published, she would give me a copy of it and asked me to sign a document to give consent. After not hearing anything more, I guessed she'd decided not to publish it, but she obviously changed her mind. I don't know who sent it. The postmark is from Winton Abbot.'

****

A week later, Belle and Milton visited Peace Haven, invited by Cherie. 'I'm so glad you could come—I want to show you something.'

She brought the tea trolley in with fresh scones up to Annie's standard, topped with Cherie's strawberries and dollops of cream. She took a book off the trolley.

'You wouldn't believe this, Belle. See this book—it's part of the curriculum for my Masters in Social Work which I have almost completed!'

There it was again, her book— Belle's Story.

'Oh Cherie, that's amazing. I didn't know that was going to happen, but I'd gave Miriam full permission to use my story for whatever she felt was necessary to get the message across.'

'I know—I sent you a copy. Did you receive it a week ago? I thought I'd surprise you.'

'Yes, and I was blown away and didn't know who sent it. I didn't think it got published in the end, as I didn't hear back from Miriam.'

'Often this kind of literature doesn't go into print for years after the event until it is finally recognised as significantly important to a cause.'

Milton turned to Cherie. 'What do you think is the main point to Belle's Story, Cherie, as a person who has been trained in empowering the lonely, lost and broken-hearted?'

'What I learned from both of you is this; no matter what the circumstances, healing takes place in an environment of nurturing, unconditional love and selfless concern for others—or altruism. Most of all, I learned that we are as sick as our secrets, and those things that were done in the darkness lose their power over us when they are brought out into the light.'

Tears of joy rolled down Belle's cheeks. She extracted an embroidered, cotton handkerchief from her pocket, wiped her eyes and choked back the tears as she spoke.

'Cherie, we know without a doubt that you and Lyon are the right people to take over Peace Haven from Annie and Murray, just as Annie and Murray were the right ones to replace us when we retired.'

EPILOGUE

Cherie picked up the book with a puzzled expression. 'There's one thing I didn't grasp about the book—there is an image of a broken web on the first page.'

Belle picked up the book and turned to the image, trying to put the message into words.

'During my grief therapy sessions, Miriam explained the process to me like this.'

'God says that we can only love others to the degree that we love and accept ourselves. So when we love others, they, in turn, can pass this on to others. It all has a snowball effect.'

'But where does the broken web come into it?' Cherie asked again.

'The woman could not see her life clearly through her own eyes initially, as her perspective had been damaged and twisted through the wreckage of her past. Her life had become entangled like a spider's web, full of self-deception. When transformation and truth entered her life, the web broke, and she was able to see her life clearly, with a pure and true vision.'

Cherie sat pensively for a moment. 'I see what you mean—it all slowly unravels until the tangled web becomes broken by the light of truth—set free.'

'You've got it, Cherie—thank God you've finally got it.'

KEEP IN TOUCH

Please visit me on my website and sign up to my mailing list to hear about new releases and giveaways.
I would love you to leave a review on your preferred reading platform.
Thank you!

Website : patriciasnelling.

Books by Author:

When Hope Went South (Dart River Novel #1)

Jessie's High Country Heart (Dart River Novel #2)

Mack The Good Shepherd (Dart River Novel #3)

Missing On Kawau

Broken Web (Peace Haven Series#1)

Unshakable (Peace Haven Series#2) Published as Rescue Net 2017